Before We Were Perfect

A

Dramedy

By Award Winning Author
S.D. Moore
Illustrated by Kostovski Nikola

Published by
MoonLeaf Publishing
Henderson, Nevada
Publication date Jan, 2018

© *2017 S.D. Moore. All rights reserved.*

No part of this novella may be reproduced, stored in a retrieval system, or transmitted by any means without the written permission of the author or publisher.

ISBN-13: 978-0-9997612-0-5 (sc)
ISBN-13: 978-0-9997612-1-2 (h)
ISBN-13: 978-0-9997612-2-9 (e)

Cover production by Pixon Designz
Images conceived and directed by S.D. Moore
Illustrated by Kostovski Nikola

FOREWORD

Before We Were Perfect is a dramatic comedy. Although the story contains lots of humor, there are some dramatic moments inspired by events related to the author's military experience.

Enjoy!

In dedication to my bud, 66th Rescue Pilot Captain Karl P. Youngblood who was one of twelve souls that perished in a late night mid-air helicopter crash near Nellis Air Force Base, NV on Sep 3rd, 1998.

Rest in power brothers in arms.

Read more about this incident in the Afterword.

Part One

Julz Havreaux is the first of her sisters to arrive at their tattoo shop this morning. She turns on all of the lights before laying out trays of snacks that her mother prepared for a celebration at the shop. At twenty-five years old, she is the second oldest of four sisters and one of the most talented tattoo artists in Flagstaff, Arizona. Some say she is one of the best in the south-west region. Her natural talents also extend to tinkering with technology and robotics, but her first love is bringing dreams to life on a canvas.

She turns on the lights in the hall. The robot dog she created years ago as class project lights up when it sees her. "Morning Abigail." Julz says.

The robot dog responds in a childlike automaton voice, *"Morning Abigail!"*

"Today, I promise that I'm going to fix that repeat error in your system." Julz says.

Julz stops to check herself out in a large mirror. She fluffs up her long soft curly hair; a gift from her ebony mother. She touches up her lipstick and then flashes the gift of her ivory father's smile. She sees a note from her sister lying on a table.

"Today is the big day. Woo hoo! Jaxx"

Cosmetic Surgeon, Dr. Jaxxelle Havreaux or Jaxx for short, is the oldest of the sisters. She is only twenty-seven, but her father used to say that she is the most level headed one of the bunch. Jaxx had to step up to help her Mom with her sisters after her father died. She's a woman who is all about her family, her business and her money; sometimes not in that order. She convinced her art inclined sisters to get a degree in Practical Nursing so that they could be best equipped to help out with the more complicated procedures at the tattoo shop. Plus, they will have another skill to fall back on during a down turn in the economy. Jaxx borrowed hundreds of thousands of dollars to create a high tech, state of the art tattoo parlor with a cosmetic surgery center for minimally invasive body modifications. The center also includes several comfortable recovery rooms.

The two youngest sisters, twenty-two-year-old Jadelyn (Jade) and twenty-one-year-old Joelle (Joe) are the wild natured ink masters of the Havreaux brood. Sometimes the difference in age between them and their older sisters makes Joe and Jade feel more like offspring of their big sisters than their younger siblings.

The sister's dearly departed father James had a thing for J-names. Their mom Connie thought it was a cute thing to do so she went along with it. As adults the four siblings agreed to merge their talents to open Flagstaff, Arizona's major tattoo shop called Wicked Sisters Ink & More. Today is the grand opening of their new body modifications wing. Now the sisters will be able to help clients achieve their desired state of perfection.

Shop assistants Daisy and Terra arrive.

"Morning Julz!" They sing out in unison.

"Morning ladies."

Jaxx, Jade and Joe arrive.

"Morning everyone!" The arriving sisters sing out.

"Hey what's with the food?" Joe asks.

"Mom sent over sausage, cheese and crackers trays for our new wing opening. The skinny ones are reindeer dogs. The medium ones are Kielbasa and the large ones are Polish sausages. She even sent over her ceramic covered cast iron sauce pots to put the dips in too." Julz says.

"Awesome! I'm starving." Jade says.

"Me too!" Daisy says as she grabs a plate.

Joe pours a jar of cheese sauce into a plastic serving bowl and then sticks a plastic spoon in the dip.

"Joe!" Julz shouts.

"What? Nobody wants to mess around with mom's fancy, smancy sauce pots anyway. Plus, it's a pain trying to get the little ladle around the pot's handle." Joe says.

"I thought mom was coming by to set up this stuff." Jade says.

"No she has an appointment. She'll meet us at the book signing for that horror author." Julz says.

"Horror isn't my thing so I'll pass, but would you mind getting me one of those naked moonlight t-shirts if you see one? I've been working out so my abs will look great under the dancing lights this year." Joe asks.

"Ditto on the horror thing, but get me a shirt too. If the dancing lights are out I'm heading over there to dance nekkid baby!" Jade says as she does a little shoulder rocking dance.

"I'm going to dance naked too." Terra says as she starts dancing behind the reception desk.

"One of us will get the t-shirts, but I'll pass on the dancing naked thing." Julz says.

The ladies do a fake pout with their lips as each of them tries to encourage Julz to go dancing under the southern Aurora Borealis.

"Come on sis. Come on sis. Come on sis" Joe says as she playfully dances.

"Yeah come twerk nude with us under the dancing lights." Jade says as she twerks.

Jaxx interrupts the crew. "Well, count me in on the book signing. I always wanted to attend one of those things. I did the naked dancing thing last year ha-ha, so I'm good."

Daisy looks out of the front window.

"Hey your uncle just pulled up."

A rather attractive middle aged man wearing a flat top gambler's hat gets out of large red pickup truck. The sign painted on the side of the truck says,

Sumner's Industrial Construction. Sumner Havreaux enters the ink shop. The ladies stop dancing and greet him.

He speaks with a relaxed Cajun drawl. "Good morning fam-lay."

"Hey Uncle Sum." The sisters sing out in unison.

"How y'all doin?" He says.

He slowly walks in and makes a line straight to Daisy.

Jaxx leans close to Julz and whispers, "Uh-oh, there he goes straight to Daisy. Messin' with Unc is a good way to catch a case of his Bayou blues."

Julz snickers softly. "Ain't that the truth."

Sumner removes his hat and then smooths down his straight silver and sandy hair. He uses his fingers to slick down his mustache and goatee before speaking to Daisy.

"I haven't seen you in a while gurl. How you been doin'?"

"Good."

"Are you switching businesses? I thought that you owned the Bayou Blues Club."

He hands her his new business card. Daisy briefly looks at the card.

"I still do, but I recently expanded my business interests. I just started my own construction comp-nee. Look-a here cher, you should holler at me sometime. You wanna join me if the dancing lights show up?" I got top shelf dranks at the ready.

"I don't know."

"You know what we call a beautiful, voluptuous gurl like you where I'm from in Louisiana?"

"No. What?" Daisy asks.

"A thick ole bowl of honey."

Daisy blushes and giggles. "Stop it Sumner! You're a mess. Besides I heard that you're a bad boy." She says.

"I may have done some thangs to make the Devil blush, but this here bad boy will always be good to you." He says.

Daisy giggles and gives Sumner a timid smile.

Joe interrupts. "Is that a new truck? Your business must be doing pretty good Uncle Sum." She asks.

"Yeah. You like it?"

"It's sweet!!" She says.

"Ya mama said that you needed to have a busted light on a sign and a hole fixed so I put y'all in the family express lane."

Jaxx walks over and gives him a hug. "Thanks Uncle Sum." Jaxx says.

"You know that I always got y'all covered." He says.

Suddenly the front door flings open. A heavy sweating junkie holding a gun bursts into the lobby of the ink shop.

"Give up the money and drugs and nobody gets hurt!"

The ladies, who look more annoyed than frightened immediately become quiet. Sumner silently observes the robber as he looks for his opportunity to take the thief down.

Jaxx speaks up. "You must've missed the sign out front? We only accept cards and checks, but no cash! Aaannd we only use drugs to numb the skin, but you can't get high off of that stuff man! If you want the hard stuff, go to Dr. Okinashi's office in the building next door!" She says with attitude.

"Wait this isn't Dr. O's place?" The robber asks.

"Nope!" Julz says.

"My mistake. You skanks better give me your purses then or there will be some fireworks in this place; starting with the curly haired one standing over there." The robber nods towards Julz.

Julz speaks in a stern voice. "I'll give you Abigail-bad-pistachios!"

The robber nods towards Julz as he speaks. "What's wrong with her? Is she having a fit or something?"

Suddenly, a knee-high metal four wheeled robot dog wearing a collar that says Abigail rolls up and stops in front of the robber. It examines the man holding the gun.

"Is this one of those expensive floor cleaners? I'll take it too." The robber asks.

The little robot dog raises its head. It squeals in a childlike automaton voice *"Bad pistachios"* as its metal head lunges up and forward slamming hard into the thief's crotch. The thief screams in pain. "Ugghhh!"

As the robber starts to collapse forward, Jade grabs one of the cast iron sauce pots sitting next the food and smacks the thief in the side of his head. Joe uses an iron pot to smack the gun from his hand. Each sister grabs a cast iron sauce pot and goes berserk hitting, stomping and kicking the guy. The robber rolls on the floor screaming as the sisters pummel him with the small iron sauce pots.

Uncle Sumner can barely control his laughter as he rushes over to help the ladies.

"Hahahahaha! Alright-alright ladies I think this idiot has had enough. *Bad pistachios!* Lord have mercy. *Hahahahaha!*" Sumner laughs hard.

He grabs some zip-ties that he uses to clamp wires together to hog-tie the bloodied bandit's hands and feet behind him. He speaks to the robber while he ties him up.

"Now you can see why they call my nieces wicked sisters. My brother's Cajun crazy runs through their veins. Ya lucky they didn't kill ya." Sumner laughs loudly. He leans in close to whisper in the robber's ear. "Trust me you gone wish they had."

"Julz lucky for us that you programed Abigail to do that trick." Jaxx says.

"It's the high school science project that keeps on giving." Julz says.

Daisy calls the police.

"Well the authorities are coming so I think that I'll get to work on that sign. Do you ladies have this robber situation under control?" Sumner Asks.

"Yeah Unc; we got this. If he so much as flinches he'll get another sauce pot beat down." Joe says as she slaps a cast iron sauce pot into the palm of her hand.

Terra steps forward to lead Sumner to the sign. "The sign and hole are over here in the waiting area. The sign is supposed to read Wicked Sisters Ink & More, but the lights burned out from the "k" in Wicked to the face representing the "o" in More." She says.

"Alright I'll work on it in your meeting room." He says.

Daisy walks towards the front door to lock it, but a customer walks in before she reaches the entrance.

A raven haired young woman with very pale skin, ruby red lips, wearing a tight black dress and short black evening gloves walks in. The woman looks down at the bloodied, hog tied man and a gun lying on the floor; then looks up at Jade holding a sauce pot.

"Tweaker thief?" The woman asks in a deep sultry tone.

"Yep." Jade responds.

"My name is Sharnia Valdana. I have a consultation appointment with Dr. Jaxxelle Havreaux."

"I'm she, but in light of the current situation on the floor you may want to reschedule."

"It looks like you ladies have the matter under control. I don't mind if you don't mind." Sharnia says.

Julz hands the woman a tablet with intake paperwork displayed on the screen. "Please follow me to the back. Would you like some hors'doeuvres and or bottled water?"

"No thank you." Sharnia says as she casually steps over the legs of the man laying on the floor.

"Jaxx we got this dude." Joe says.

"Yeah, you handle the patient while we tweaker-sit. It's in his best interest not to do or say anything else stupid or so help me - bam!" Jade says as she slams her fist into the palm of her hand.

"Plus the police just pulled up." Daisy says.

"Okay." Jaxx heads to the back.

"I'm Officer Gallagher and this is Officer Parks from Flagstaff PD. I take it this tied up individual is the guy?"

"Yes sir." Joe says.

"Is that his weapon laying over there?"

"Yes sir." Joe responds.

"I'm going to take your statements on my Tab-corder. Look at the spot on the screen, state your name, address and phone number. After that give your statement and answer follow-up questions as needed. I'll start with you." He says as he holds the Tab-corder in front of Joe.

"My name is Joelle Havreaux." She gives her address and phone number.

"Please tell me what happened and how the suspect sustained his injuries."

"The dude busted in here waving a gun. He demanded drugs and money. Luckily we caught him off guard and we were able to knock his gun away. He sustained his injuries as we struggled to detain him for the authorities. That's the end of my statement."

"Okay. Please use your finger to sign your name at the bottom of the screen. Would you like a print or email copy of your statement?"

"Both."

"Okay please type your email address here and hit send."

He prints out a copy of the statement then hands it to Joe. Gallagher runs through the same procedure with Jadelyn, Daisy, and Terra. Sumner steers clear of the scene by working in a rear office.

"Well, it looks like we're done here. Have a great day everyone." The police haul the robber out of the building.

Jaxx joins Julz and the patient. Jaxx reaches out her hand to Sharnia.

"Let me properly introduce myself. I'm doctor Jaxxelle Havreaux. Sorry about that mess ma'am."

"Oh no problem. This is the unfortunate age that we are living in. Havreaux - does your family hail from France?"

"It's Creole. My family transplanted here after a very destructive hurricane. Now, how can we help you?" Jaxx asks.

"Currently, I don't have any tatts or piercings. I'm not sure that what I want is actually possible to create."

"You never know. We've done some pretty radical body art work. Lay it on us." Julz says.

"I am a professional mistress. I want to…"

Julz cuts her off. "Ma'am, did you..."

"Please call me Sharnia."

"Sharnia did you say that you are a professional mistress? I'm not passing judgement. I just need to make sure that I heard you correctly." Julz says.

"Yes. That's correct. You may be more familiar with the term Dominatrix."

"Oh I see. Go on." Jaxx says.

"Well I would like a black widow spider tattooed on my puu-twawny."

"Your vagina. Okay go on. Jaxx says.

"My puu-twawny will be waxed of course, but after I heal I would like the hair to be sculpted to conform to the body of the spider. A laser should be used to permanently remove any unnecessary hair."

"Okay, no problem we can do that in two stages." Julz says.

"I also want the spider to have two ruby red jeweled eyes on top that will be in the form of a piercing. I also want the entrance of my puu-twawny modified with an implant at the base of the entrance that will feel like a narrow tongue. It will have one fang on each side of the tongue. The fangs should be designed to create a bit of discomfort when a member rubs against it."

"Discomfort for a male's member?" Jaxx asks.

"Yes. My companions prefer pain with their pleasure." Sharnia says.

"I just wanted to make sure that I get it right."

"Of course. Do you think that what I want can be accomplished?" Sharnia asks.

"Yes. We can do it. You will have to stay in our recovery center for four days after the implant procedure is done. We want to make sure that everything is done to prevent rejection or infection. We can cut down on rejection if I can get a sample of fat cells from your labia majora commonly called the vaginal lips so that an organic implant can be grown. Would you prefer synthetic or organic? Synthetic is less expensive and riskier."

"Organic of course. That way the implant will easily merge with my anatomy. It will be part of me."

"Exactly. The fat cells can be grown and molded into the shape of a tongue and fangs. The new part can be brought to maturity in three weeks. It will cost $2500 to use an organic part instead of a synthetic one. Would you be ready to give a cell sample today?" Jaxx says.

"Of course." Sharnia replies.

"I can perform the vaginal modification procedure and piercing three weeks after you get your tattoo. The price will be $2500 for the organic implant and $2000 for the modifications. It's $1000 per day for around the clock care, $150 for the piercing, $600 for the jewelry and $750 for the design and tattoo. That comes to $10,000. Will that be check, atm card or charge?" Jaxx asks.

Sharnia reaches into her purse and pulls out a plastic card. "Please use my atm card. Should I pay at the front desk?"

"You can use this machine right here." Jaxx slides a card machine towards Sharnia. She runs her card and Jaxx hands her receipt.

Please follow Julz to examination room ten so that I can get that fat cell sample." Jaxx says.

Julz leads her to the exam room. She hands Sharnia a paper robe and a large paper covering.

"Please undress, put on the robe with the opening to the front, put your feet in the stirrups and cover your lower half with this cloth. Dr. Havreaux will be right with you."

"Okay." Sharnia replies.

"Alright Sharnia I'm going to numb a small area of your left inner vaginal lip. Then I'm going to take tiny sample. Okay?"

"Okay. I'm ready." Sharnia says.

Jaxx finishes the quick procedure.

"All done. I'll send this out to the lab." Jaxx carries away the sample.

Julz flashes a muted smile. She knows that "The Lab" really means that Jaxx is taking the tissue to a secret room where she illegally grows parts for body implants. It's a trick that Jaxx learned from her ex-boyfriend who was a geneticist. She discovered that following a formula to grow parts in a lab is very similar to following a complicated recipe. It's hard at first, but beautiful things can be created with practice.

Sharnia turns to Julz. "Is it possible to do the tattoo tomorrow?"

"Absolutely. I'll work up the design and one of the artists will ink it tomorrow. Meet me in the doctor's office after you get dressed." Julz says.

After Sharnia enters the office Julz walks her over to a medical mannequin. "Sharnia, I'm going to create a design for the tattoo. Please show me on the vaginal area of the mannequin where you want the spider's legs to begin and end."

Sharnia works with Julz to create the design.

They conclude the appointment and Jaxx walks Sharnia towards the front door.

Sharnia looks done at the floor. "Look at that. You ladies already cleaned up the mess and have the place looking brand new. I knew that I picked the right place. See you tomorrow." She says as she saunters out of the door.

Jaxx locks the door.

"Now how is everyone doing after that craziness this morning?" Jaxx says.

"I'm still a little freaked, but good." Daisy says.

"Easy and steady." Terra says.

Jaxx turns towards her sisters. "How about you guys?"

"I'm pissed and freaked, but cool." Joelle says.

"Ditto." Says Jade.

"I'm straight." Julz says.

"Good. I'm glad everyone is okay. Since one of Dr. O's patients tried to rob us, we're going to keep the door locked and only take appointments. We're also going to get a new no drugs or money sign with pictures on it.

"Do we have any other appointments this morning?" Jaxx asks.

Daisy looks at the appointment book before responding.

"We only have two appointments. Jade has a guy who wants his son's name on his arm and Joe has Prepper Dan who wants a medium sized head of an eagle wearing a red, white and blue bandana on his shoulder." She says.

"It'll take me an hour to draw up that spider tatt and then I'm going over to meet up with mom." Julz says, but honestly she wasn't feeling good.

"That sounds like easy stuff. Jade and Joe after you finish up the next two tatt appointments close up shop and everyone take the rest of the day off with triple pay for the day. Terra and Daisy reschedule all late afternoon appointments. Oh and here's two hundred dollars each to go relax a bit." Jaxx says.

Sumner emerges from the back carrying a large sign.

"Ladies I fixed your sign."

He hangs it up on the wall. "A few of the wires weren't properly connected and they came loose. I also noticed that the blinking lights for the skull's eyes in the center of the "o" were never installed, but I took care of it. I even got the hat the skull's wearing to light up. Here, I'll turn off the overhead lights so that you can check it out. Voila! Wicked Sisters Ink & More lights up. Darn it's almost perfect. Only one of lights in the eyes is blinking! I'll take it down and fix it." He says.

"Nah, you can leave it Uncle Sum." Julz says.

She grabs the hands of Jade and Joe. She tosses a warm smile and nod to Jaxx, Terra and Daisy. All of the ladies stand shoulder to shoulder clasping hands.

"Between the craziness in this place and our crazy lives, it's a perfect fit for us." Julz says.

Part Two

Julz and Jaxx meet up with their mother at the bookstore.

"Hi mom!" Each sister greets their mom with a kiss on the cheek.

"I see Joe and Jade bowed out on the book signing huh? Those girls always hated horror stuff. How'd the new wing opening go?"

"It was crazy, but we handled it." Jaxx says.

"Good! Isn't this a lovely day? Just when I thought the weather on this beautiful fall day couldn't get any better, Mother Nature bats her eye lashes and paints the mountains with a gorgeous rainbow. Look at the smiling faces walking around downtown. They can feel it too. We have sunshine, melting snow and an autumn rainbow. It makes standing outside in this long line heavenly." Connie Havreaux says.

Jaxx rolls her eyes before speaking. "Geez Mom you're starting to sound like a hippie."

"Can't you girls feel the positive energy tingling through you?"

"What I feel tingling through me is the urge to pee. And watching the water from melting snow trickle between the cobblestones we're standing on ain't helping." Jaxx says.

Julz chuckles.

"It wouldn't hurt you to gain some appreciation for nature Jaxx." Connie says as she locks arms with her daughter Julz.

"I've been attending Mindfulness sessions to support my friend, I think it's rubbing off on me. You should try it Jaxx." Connie says.

"The only thing I'm gonna try to do is not wet my pants. I can't believe this many people are in line for a book signing. Who knew that D.B. Greene had such a huge following in Flagstaff, Arizona? Sheesh! You guys hold my book while I find a toilet." Jaxx hands her book to Julz and then trots off.

"This line is pretty frickin' long Mom. I like reading his stuff, but whoa!" Julz says.

"Are you going to be ok dear? If standing is going to be too much for you, go wait across the street at Better Monday's Coffee Shop. I'll get the author to sign your book too."

"No I'm feeling pretty good Mom. Besides, I always wanted to do the whole book signing thing."

"I just don't want you to overdo it."

"Mom I'm good. You really worry too much about me. Ooo! Look the bookstore has those glow in the dark - I'm a Naked Moonlight Dipper sweatshirts." Julz says.

"Oh I can't believe people are still doing that." Connie says.

"Come on Mom! You know that you used to chase the dancing Aurora lights when you were younger."

"Yeah, but in my day if people went au naturale they certainly didn't advertise that they did it on the front of a t-shirt."

Three young women walk by Connie and Julz wearing - I'm a Naked Moonlight Dancer shirts.

"See that Julz? A bunch of hussies on a high wire ringing a dinner bell."

Julz shakes her head, closes her eyes and sighs. "Wow Mom! You need to let your hair down. Good the line is moving faster. Just a few more steps and we'll be standing inside."

Jaxx rejoins her family. She's holding a black t-shirt up to her chest. "Look, I just bought an - I'm a Naked Moonlight Dancer shirt. Here, I got one for the two of you and Jade and Joe too. Here's yours Mom."

Their Mom rolls her eyes.

Julz laughs hard. "Hahahahahahahahaha! Thanks hussie."

"What? What'd I miss?" Jaxx asks.

Julz continues to snicker.

The ladies finally make it inside of the bookstore. Connie can barely contain her excitement. "Ooo, ooo, ooo I see him! Connie says.

"Take it down a notch mom. We don't want to look like crazed fans."

"Oh he's really good looking. He looks better than the pic on the back of his book. I think that he's in your age range Julz. Toss your hair a bit so that you'll look like a windblown magazine model." Connie says.

"No!" Julz says while rolling her eyes.

"If you don't like him my friend has a son around your age. I think that he's a doctor. I heard that he's very nice."

"Mom stop it." Julz says sternly.

"I thought that he would look a lot more hardcore. He's cute, but kind of plain looking for a horror author." Jaxx says.

Julz stands in line behind her mother and sister. She pauses to shake her left leg. She walks a little further then pauses to shake her leg again. Julz can feel her leg starting to do what she refers to as the numbing thing that now plagues her almost every day.

Jaxx notices that Julz is having issues with her leg. She whispers to her sister, "Want me to get the cane from Mom?"

"*No!* Can't I have a tiny moment of normalness?"

"Ok wannabe normal woman. Maybe you should go over to the reading area and sit on one of those sofas before Mom starts freaking out." Jaxx whispers.

"I think I'm going to be ok. It's actually feeling better now." Julz whispers.

The ladies make it to the signing table. The author sits in front of a life size cardboard mannequin of himself holding a copy of his horror novel, *Night of the Leapers*. Connie's hands shake a little at her excitement to meet the author. She finds herself stuttering as she speaks. "Oh-uh-um Mr. Greene. It's such a pleasure. I'm uh."

Julz interrupts her mother's embarrassing introduction. "D.B. please excuse my mother. She is a huge fan of your work."

Her mother silently offers her book to the author for his signature.

"Who do I make this out to?" D.B. asks.

Her mother stands there silently staring at the author. Julz replies for her mother. "Please autograph the book to Connie Havreaux. That's spelled, H-a-v-r-e-a-u-x."

The author autographs the book and then hands it back to Connie. "Thank you for reading Night of the Leapers." Connie nods her head up and down.

"Thank you. Come along Mother." Julz takes her mother by the arm and they begin to walk away.

D.B. calls to Julz. "Wait. Don't you want me to sign your book miss?"

"Yeah. I forgot about that." Julz says.

She swiftly turns around, but this time during her pivot her entire right leg goes numb from her hip down to her foot. She begins to fall forward towards the author. She reaches out her arms to try to break her fall on a stack of books, but the books on top of the stacks slide forward; tossing Julz onto more stacks of books sitting on the floor. The weight of her body causes the rest of the books to tumble forward. Julz quickly finds herself body surfing stacks of books right pass the author and two book shelves.

The expressions on the faces of the customers in the bookstore falls between shock, concern and hand over mouth shame-filled laughter.

D.B. Greene rushes to her aide. He stares at the beautiful dark auburn haired mess lying in front of him and smiles. He begins to lift Julz from the floor.

"Oh my goodness miss are you alright?" He stops moving, blushes and then turns his head away after he sees that her breast is exposed.

"Um-um, you better close your jacket Miss. Your shirt ripped and your breast is exposed." He says.

"Oh pardon the bad tattoo on my boob. I've been meaning to get that butterfly fixed. Now stop freaking out and help me up." She snaps.

"And I thought that you were just another normal girl..." He says as he helps her up.

The two of them speak a line from a book in unison, "...but a crazy person can't play sane for long." They both snicker.

"I see that you read Shelby Camron." D.B. says.

"And you do too. I guess that makes you ok for a horror writer."

Her mother and sister rush to Julz's side.

"Oh I'm sorry for the mess Mr. Greene. I'll pay for any damages." Connie says.

"Pay him? He should be grateful that we don't sue him for this death trap of books he has laying around. Come on Julz!" Jaxx says sternly.

Julz looks at the author and shakes her head no as she silently mouths, "We're not gonna sue."

Julz's mother and sister help her walk to the door.

D.B. motions to his friend and agent. "What in the hell just happened Youngblood?"

"Remember when I gave you the business card of Wicked Sisters Ink & More and told you that they're the best tattoo artists within one hundred miles who can fix that tatt on your back?"

"Yeah."

"Well those two beautiful young women with smart mouths are half of the wicked sisters."

"Oh. That's not good." D.B. says

"The lady who talked about suing you is the oldest one and owner; and butterfly boob does a lot of their specialty artwork. I swear those two women are gifted."

"It looks like I'm screwed Youngblood."

"Nah. Even female monsters have a heart. I'm sure you'll come up with some way to charm them." Youngblood says before patting D.B. on the shoulder and walking away.

Part Three

The next morning Julz wakes up with extremely tired muscles, aches and pains in areas that she never felt aches in before. She looks at her body in the bathroom mirror and shakes her head as she uses her very pale hands to explore the bruises on her shoulders and forearms. Julz lifts up her tank top and sees more bruises. "Oh my God! I even have bruises under my boobs! Seriously?" She yells.

Julz showers and dresses into some sweats. She decides that in light of the fallout from falling the day before, she also has to deal with autoimmune disease issues. She decides that today will officially be take it easy Monday. She prepares some organic pizza with onions, organic ham and Cotija cheese; uncaps some organic ginger ale. She decides to work from home.

"Time for another test run of mechanical mobile me."

She walks over to her desk, flips on the computer and logs into the shop's WSI portal. The makeshift robotic avatar she comes online. Julz adjusts the camera lens to view the interior of the tattoo shop. She uses a remote control move the avatar around the shop. She checks out her avatar in a mirror. She can see her face on the screen of a tablet that sits near the top of the five-and-a-half-foot robot. Just above the screen is a high tech lens with multi-rotational capabilities. When she zooms out, an image of a painted plywood cutout of a blue haired cyclops wearing purple rubber gloves and a white lab coat stares back. She slightly rolls the robot left and right modeling her mechanical creation in the mirror. She turns the avatar to left and sees assistants Daisy and Terra standing near the reception desk. She, could carry on straight to her first appointment, decides to catch up on the shop's gossip.

"Mic check. Morning Daisy. Morning Terra. What's the shop scoop ladies?"

"Jaxx and Jade are implanting three rows of metal spikes in the forehead of one of the Big Bayou Boys in room 1."

Julz rolls her eyes. "The triple B's huh? You can take the gators out of the Bayou, but you can't take the swamp out of the gators." Julz says.

"Joe is working on Leslie Beagle."

"Isn't that the former leader of the mean girls from your high school who now has three kids by three different guys who swears that she was cheated out of being the Queen of the Fair?" Julz says.

"Yeah her. She's getting a horizontal row of three of her face pics with the words Beagle-Juice written underneath each image as a tramp stamp." Terra says.

"Wow! She's still at it! Oh well I guess the stamp is like calling for Bloody Mary in a mirror; you gotta say the name three times before anyone comes sooo..." Julz says.

"Ewww! Hahahaha!" Terra and Daisy say in unison before laughing.

Daisy elbows Terra before whispering to her. "Hey this one will get Julz going." Daisy says.

"Oh and this afternoon Joe and Jade are doing matching tatts on the four guys from that Eve's Helper Infomercial." Daisy says.

"Who?"

"You know the guys who came up with those sani liners with a disposable computer chip in them that sends a message to a user's phone to alert a woman when she has started her flow. You're pretty tech savvy Julz. What are your thoughts on that?" Terra asks.

They watch Julz's face on the screen of her avatar as she squints her eyes and scrunches her eyebrows into a frown before she responds.

"Oh don't get me started about those guys who came up with that panties full of nightmares. Now a user will have to keep her phone charged up to prevent a friggin' mess. I saw a video of some poor woman who got tasered at the airport because one of those things gave off a bad signal in her nether region. News reports said she was convulsing and pissing herself on the airport's floor.

Man, talk about having a hot box – ouch! What gets me is that I actually patented something that actual scientists reference for their inventions and these guys end up with a famous TV show for inventing a hoo-hah monitor. I just can't anymore!"

Terra and Daisy stand at the counter roaring with laughter.

Terra speaks through happy tears, "Oh Julz you're a nut! Hey a delivery guy dropped these off for you." Terra points to a vase with two dozen multicolored roses.

Julz examines the flowers before speaking through the tablet's speaker. "Who are they from?"

She watches Daisy fish for the card. "The card says, Julz I hope all is well. At your service. David Greene."

"David Greene? Oh that's that writer guy. He probably feels bad about the spill I took at his book signing." Julz says.

"Yeah I heard about that at the pub last night." Daisy says.

"Wuh-what?" Julz demands.

Daisy hunches her shoulders as she speaks, "Hey in a small town like this, shade travels fast on social media."

Julz rolls her eyes before responding.

"I can't deal with this right now. It's almost time for my special design appointment. I'll wait in a room until the client arrives."

"Oh he arrived twenty minutes early. Mr. Smith is in room 4." Terra says.

"What? You should've led with that!" Julz says.

Julz moves her avatar through the exam room corridor. She rolls down hallway until her avatar arrives in front of room 4. She pushes the avatar through the doorway of the room. She sees a man wearing a knit cap lying on his right side with his back to her. She notices a large tattoo drawn across his entire upper back. She also sees large burn and stitches scars on his left side and waist that make parts of his skin look like a patch work quilt made of swaths of wrinkled leather. She disregards his huge scars

"Hello sir. Sorry to keep you waiting. My name is Julz. I'm the artist who will create your design. Please don't be alarmed by my appearance. I work from home via an avatar. Would you like something to drink?"

Abigail the dog robot rolls in carrying a refrigerated bucket by a rope hanging from the jaws of her mouth. She displays bottles of flavored and unflavored water for the customer. The little bot extends her neck and head upward by over a foot to allow the client to reach the drinks.

"No thank you."

Abigail retracts her head and rolls away.

"Alright, let me take a look at the issue. My notes say that you want to have your tatt corrected. I'm looking at your back. I see an image of the Aurora Borealis above a full moon, below that is a night time lake scene surrounded by a forest. Beneath that is the word Lepers. What do you want me to do add oozing boils or maybe a horde of zombie lepers?"

Without rolling over to speak face, to face with Julz the man says, "Zombie lepers that's funny and possibly redundant, but no. I need the word corrected to read Leapers. That's spelled, L-e-a-p-e-r-s. Some idiot wasn't paying attention so now I'm left with lepers under a full moon."

"Hmm. I need to think about this for a beat sir."

"I don't want to have most of it removed. I just want to add the letter - a." The man says.

"Let me work something up. I'll have Daisy call you in two to three days ok?"

"Okay. Oh and I also want my left shoulder, arm, side, and leg covered in a warrior tatt, but I'm torn between a gladiator or something like it." He says.

"We do a lot of gladiator tatts. Since it's a large area, I'll come up with some options."

"Okay." He says.

"Daisy will be in touch."

Julz rolls her avatar out of the room. She stops her avatar at the front desk.

"Hey Daisy ping me if you need me."

"Will do Julz."

Julz returns her avatar to its charging port.

She puts on virtual reality gloves and slips on her V/R goggles to bring up the image of Mr. Smith's misspelled tattoo in virtual reality. She uses her fingers, hands, and eyebrows to manipulate the commands on the screen. She commands the program to vertically lift the image and the human canvas. A copy of the client's back with tattoo rises and stands erect like a hard sheet of paper. Julz goes to work sketching out ideas in virtual reality.

Julz uses her fingers to paint broad colorful lines. She moves a drawing wand to create more intricate lines. Julz swipes her hand to erase everything that she just created. She tries a new idea with tiny forest animals, but wipes that image away too. Julz tries over and over and over again, but nothing feels right. She needs to clear her head. She sighs with frustration before shutting things down for the day.

Part Four

The next day Julz answers a knock at her door of her apartment. It's Jaxx and Joe dressed in Halloween costumes.

"Hey Sis. I thought that I would drop off the flowers that the author sent you." Joe says

"Thanks! Your superhero get-up is sweet Jaxx! Joe you look so 80's in that neon green lace head band and tight skirt. And you even have cute pouch for your phone. Are you Madonna or Lauper?"

"I'm just an 80's girl." Joe replies.

"Your costumes are a little conservative compared to last year." Julz says

"I'm in the mood to play it a little low key this year." Jaxx says.

"Where's Jade?"

"She went to the movies with Scott." Joe says.

Jaxx looks at Joe's face. She licks her thumb and begins to smooth down Joe's eyebrows.

Joe jerks her head away from her sister's wet thumb.

"*What the heck Jaxx?* "

"Your eyebrows look messy so I..."

"Geez Jaxx stop acting like Mom #2."

"But, I was just trying to help." Jaxx says.

"*Only babies need that kind of help! What are you going to do next wipe my tee-tee after I wee-wee? Cause if you do you'll see that I wear big girl panties now also known as a thong. That's right a thong!*" Joe shouts.

"You do know that thongs will cause a chapped butt crack. I'm just saying that you might want to switch it up a bit." Jaxx says.

"*Aarrgghh! Sometimes you can be ridiculous! I'll wait in the car!*" Joe shouts as she storms off.

"She's kind of moody. Anyway, since you're staying home would you mind looking at the gear that came in? The logo looks a little funny to me." Jaxx says.

"Maybe, but I just might pass through the party for a drink or two." Julz says.

"Well whatever you do Sis please, please, please be careful if you decide to go it alone. Mom will freak if something happens while you're out on the town." Jaxx says.

Jaxx joins Joe in the car and the two of them leave for the party.

Julz races over to her closet and pulls out the bunny costume that she made out of faux fur. It's grey with a heart shaped bust line. The rabbit ears mask only covers the area around her eyes and the top and tip of her nose. She marvel's at how perfect the costume looks to. She can go to a party and if her disease makes her stagger around like a drunk woman, no one will know her identity. She excitedly gets ready for the party.

Julz waits until 9 pm to take an unmanned Personal Assistant Transport (PAT) to the Bayou Blues Club. She sees people entering and leaving the party. Two of the guests leaving look like her sister Joe and one of the clients from the ink shop named Dan Mazant aka Prepper Dan. An overflow of guests spills onto the front porch. A few people toss a quick "Hey or hello" her way. She throws them a hello with the flick of her bunny hand and the nod of her head.

Julz hasn't been in night club in a while. She walks inside bopping her bunny ears to an old school 90s dance jam. She's fascinated by the two long aquatics tanks that line each side of the dance floor leading to a stage. Each tank is filled with four small live alligators. Sitting in the middle of each tank is the skeleton of Uncle Sumner's departed friends. In the left tank are the remains Braxton LaCrone and the bones of Vincent Muriel sit in the tank on the right. She heard a story that her uncle legally received the bodies of the men through their Wills. A line in each Will said, "I [insert friend's name] perform this willful act to increase Sumner Havreaux's power through the gift of my bones." That's what they call in your face Bayou Juju right there.

In front of the gator tanks she notices six dance platforms. A sign is tacked to each dance platform that says: "*Do Not Touch the Dancers. First Touch a Warning - Second Touch a Cast.*"

She likes the fun atmosphere of people dancing, drinking and flirting. Julz watches the male and female guests shake it on the risers in front of the gator tanks. It's not long before some drunk guy gets too handsy with one of the guests dancing on a platform. She watches as one the Triple Bs gets the guy's attention and then points his finger at the sign tacked to the dance platform. The guy flips off one of the Triple Bs and proceeds to reach up and grab a dancer's booty. Julz watches as a one of the Big Bayou Boys punches the guy in the gut before unnaturally twisting and bending the grabber's arm behind his back. She doesn't need to rely on her medical training to tell her that the grabber will soon need a cast. Julz shakes her head at the scene of the grabber being tossed out of the club. The other party goers continue to dance on without skipping a beat.

Julz dances with a couple of random guys then takes a break. She stands at the bar contemplating getting a drink. She's not supposed to drink with her new meds, but since she's not driving she pushes the thought out of head and orders her favorite potion; a shot of cognac with a splash of lemon-lime soda and twist of lemon. She stands in an out of the way spot to people watch while she sips her drink.

Uncle Sumner stands on stage next to the DJ's table. Sumner looks menacing wearing smoked shadowed eyes, a voodoo priest's top hat with a tiny skull sitting above crossed bones high in the center of the hat; with tiny skulls encircling the entire brim. He is holding a long wooden staff with a human skull wearing a top hat adorned with feathers sitting at the top of the staff and a six-inch silver tip at the bottom of the staff. He grabs the mic to make an announcement.

"How y'all doin' tonight? *I said how y'all doin tonight?*" He shouts.

The crowd roars with hoots, hollers and applause.

"Thank y'all for coming out this evenin'. I see a lot of new friends and many old friends who had to leave the Bayou. Now I'm gonna pour one out for those who transitioned to the great beyond due to the Cane's dirty water in our old hometown. The flood took a lot, but now we got our power back."

Shouts of "Yeah! Oh yeah!" erupt from the audience.

As we say where we come from..."

Sumner raises his wooden staff high in the air with his right hand.

"Laissez les bon temps rouler! *Let the good times roll!*" Sumner shouts into the mic.

Everyone shouts "*Woooo!*"

The music roars on.

Julz grabs her sister's arm as she walks in front of her.

"Hey Jaxx."

Jaxx examines the exposed mouth under the half faced bunny mask.

"Hey who's that? Hahaha! Julz is that you?" She gives Julz a hug.

"Surprise! Haha!"

Jaxx sniffs her sister's cup. "What are you drinking? I hope that its juice? Well I can't tell you what to do because you're a grown woman, but if you need me, text me. I have my phone on vibrate so I'll get it and swoop in and save you."

"Don't worry Jaxx I got this." Julz says.

"You seen Joe? I want to see what time she wants to leave."

"She already left."

"*What? With who?*"

"Prepper Dan."

"Oh my frickin goodness! Prepper Dan? Not that paranoidal paranoiac! I can't believe that kook is in med school. I don't know what she sees in that fruit cake."

"He is kind of hot Jaxx. Besides he's harmless paranoiac. At least we don't have to worry about anything happening to her. He's got plenty of guns and I heard that his house is like a medieval fortress."

"She should've said something before she left. I thought that I was her ride."

"She's probably still ticked about you acting like her mommy earlier."

"Yeah that was kind of messed up huh? I promise to do better." Jaxx says.

"Check your phone. Maybe Joe sent you a text." Julz says.

Jaxx checks her phone and sure enough there is a message from Joe stating that she was leaving with Dan.

"I have a message from her. Why didn't I feel the hum?"

Jaxx checks the side of her phone.

"Oh my frickin Lord! I accidently put my phone on silent! I've been off my game ever since that frickin tweaker tried to rob us. Text me if you need me." Jaxx says as she storms away.

Julz continues to dance in the corner and sip on her drink. Suddenly her eyes become blurry and soon the people in the party divide into twins. She closes her eyes for a few seconds and opens them, but she still sees two of everyone at the party. She jiggles her legs and breathes a sigh of relief that her legs aren't acting up too. She sits her drink down and attempts to dial her phone, but the numbers are too blurry. Rather than upset the guests at the party, she stands still waiting for her flare up to calm down. About a half hour later her vision clears up well enough to leave the party. She heads for the front door. She walks past several people standing outside talking on their phones.

Julz starts walking in the direction of her house. The cool evening air helps to clear her head a bit. She makes it about a quarter of block before her vision starts acting up again. She misjudges a step which causes her to slip on some ice. Her bunny costume feet peddle rapidly in place like a giant cartoon rabbit as she tries to keep from falling, but her efforts are useless as she finally plops tail down into a bank of hard refrozen snow. Julz tries to get up, but her costume is hung up on the ice. She jerks her body hard to the right to try to break free of whatever she is caught up on in the snow. She rocks and pulls until she comes unstuck and rolls over on her belly. Unfortunately, the trap drawer in her bunny suit tears on the jagged frozen snow and comes undone; exposing her partially lace covered backside. She tries to get up, but negotiating in the bunny costume has tired her out. She stops struggling to stand up.

Julz speaks aloud to herself, "Well I guess this is it. They'll find me, lying butt up in a bunny suit, frozen to death in a pile of snow."

Someone clears their throat. Soon Julz hears a man's voice speak to her.

"It's lucky for you that I saw you do that slapstick bunny flop into the snow Julz."

Julz speaks with slurry words. "Who'z zat?"

"It's me, David Greene."

"That writer dude? Oh this night can't get any worse? How did you know that it's me?" She asks.

"The butterflies on your lower butt cheek gave you away. What are the odds of encountering two women in the same town, prone to falling, who also have the same turquoise butterflies tattooed on the left side of their body?"

"Oh that's just frickin great! I've shown my 'T' and my 'A' to a perfect stranger and I didn't even get a tip. I'm like the worst broke down stripper ever. My mother will be so proud."

"Haha!" He laughs as he reaches down to lift her up.

"Come on broke down stripper. Let's get your face out of the snow." He says

David helps Julz to her feet and begins to brush the snow off of her costume. She looks at his cowboy outfit.

She tries to stand straight, wobbles a little bit. "Who are you supposed to be Tonto?" She asks.

"No I'm Jessie James, but you are thinking of the Ranger. Anyway, it's starting to snow so I'll give you a ride home."

"No thanks cowboy! I'll walk." Julz says.

"Really? Do you want to fall down again and die in the snow or maybe have some pervert come along and take advantage of an inebriated snow bunny?"

"Oh puh-lease! Like I can trust a creepy horror writer. I'll probably get Dextered or something. And I'm not nee-bree-ated neither." Julz slurs.

David purses his lips and squints his eyes as he hears her slur her words. "Ok I'll call you a PAT and I'll pay for it."

"*No! Don't do that!*" She demands.

"Why not?"

"Because if a PAT droid thinks I'm in distress it will immediately call for emergency assistance and I'll end up at the hospital. That's the last place that I want to go."

"Are you in distress?" David asks.

"No."

"Hmm? Okay give me your mother's number and I'll call her.

"*Oh hell no!* Thanks for helping me up, but like I said, I'll walk." She says.

"Well at least let me walk with you. I couldn't stand the thought of allowing you to walk off and I later find out that something happened to you."

David grabs his coat, gloves and a blanket from the backseat of his vehicle.

"Here. If I tie this blanket around your neck like so it covers your bare butt. Hahaha! Now you look like a super hero bunny."

"Fun-nee." Julz sneers.

They only walk a few steps before Julz throws up all over the front of her costume. She swoons then passes out belly up and spread eagle in the snow. This time David sweeps her up in his arms and places her on the backseat of his SUV.

He is having difficulty sliding her all of the way into his vehicle. He pushes and pulls, but the torn tail of her costume is hung up on the seatbelt latch. He gives up and rolls down the rear passenger window. He lets her bunny feet hang out of the window.

To his embarrassment one of his grandmother's church friend's is out walking her little pug on a leash.

"*David Bryan Greene*! What kind of indecent business are you up to?"

"I'm just helping out a person in need Mrs. Murdoch."

"I'm sure that's what all the weirdos say. I used to go to church with your grandmother Otherine. She would frown on this kind of foolishness. Lord rest her soul."

"Yes Mrs. Murdoch."

"What was it drugs or a roofer in that bunny's drink?"

"It's only alcohol ma'am."

"Alcohol? Well don't let me find out that you've done something freaky to that boozed up bunny in your backseat or I'll be old school comin' for ya!" She pats her cleavage a couple of times to let David know that she's packing heat.

"I would never do anything like that ma'am." He says.

"Well see that you don't." She snatches her little dog's leash. "Come on Moscatio!"

"Good night Mrs. Murdochhhhhhh." He sings.

David jumps into the driver's seat and then pulls off. Julz's bunny covered feet wave in the wind as he drives away.

*****

Joelle and Dan listen to music and dance around in his living room. He's wearing a fake blood spattered hospital surgical scrubs costume with the words Prepper Doc written in bold letters on the front of the shirt. He has a plastic Uzi strapped to his hip. Dan stops dancing.

He speaks to Joe with his slight southern drawl.

"Hey cutie I'm thirsty. You want something to drank? I got beer, ale and lager."

"Um aren't those the same thing?"

"Nawl girl."

"I'll try a lager straight out of the bottle please."

"Alll-riiight. My home girl keeping it real. Straight out the bottle coming up."

"There seem to be a lot of us post Kat transplants here." She says.

He hands Joe a brew. She takes a sip and starts dancing again. She stops when she notices some Halloween stuff and a strobe light sitting in a box.

"Those are my decorations. Look I have press on Z-scars in a kit like the fake scars I have on my arms. Here I'll put some on you and we can role play. You can be my zombie honey." He says.

"That's freaky." She thinks about it for a second. "But okay."

He presses fake Z-scars on her face.

"Okay how do I look?" She asks.

"Like a kind of drunk very hot zombie girl." He kisses her on the nose.

"Ha-ha! You're silly." She laughs.

Joe puts on the Columbian Raggaeton My People song. She turns on the strobe light and starts to do a sexy dance in the flashing lights.

"Go gurl! Go gurl! Shake that zombie thang! Come mone-nah shake that sexy thang!"

She giggles. Joe picks up the strobe light, then shines it on Dan.

"Your turn. Now you shake that sexy thang for me Prepper Doc."

"Alright, here you go gurl! Let me hit you with my male dancer moves. *Boom!*"

He starts dancing and then he abruptly stands still staring straight ahead. Joe watches as he suddenly falls to the ground and then starts writhing on the floor.

"*Dan!*" She screams.

She turns off the strobe light, then rushes to him. She can clearly see that he is having a seizure. Joe's medical training immediately kicks in. She snatches a couple of pillows from the sofa, then uses them to help roll over on his left side. She positions the pillows to keep Dan propped on his side to prevent him from aspirating any vomit.

After she rolls him she can see blood on the right side of his head. Joe let's out a sigh of relief when the seizure stops. She checks his mouth to make sure there isn't any vomit inside. After she finds nothing, Joe races to the kitchen and then grabs some paper towels. She holds the towels on the wound. She tries to revive Dan. He remains unconscious, but breathing normally.

Joe uses Dan's house phone to call for an ambulance. She grabs his keys and unlocks the front door. She notices that his head is still bleeding pretty bad. She races upstairs to the master bedroom to get some cotton towels, but when she reaches the room, a gust of wind blows open the unlocked front door and sets off the burglary alarm. It also triggers Dan's internal booby trap system which causes gates to slide out of the walls; trapping her in the bedroom. Joe is feeling frustrated that she can't help Dan or get herself out of the house. Luckily she has her cellphone in her little pouch. She calls her sister Jade.

Jade is sitting a theater next to her boyfriend Scott watching a movie. She sees her phone light up as it rings, but she ignores it. Her phone rings again, but she ignores the flashing a second time. She decides to check her phone. She sees a text from Joelle telling her that Dan had a seizure, is unconscious and that she is trapped in his bedroom. She ends the message with the word "sec."

Jade understands what her little sister means by "sec." It is their code for don't let the older sisters or mom know about an embarrassing mess. Jade shows Scott the message. The two of them hurry out of the movie theater and jump inside of Scott's car. Jade calls Joe.

"We're on our way." Jade says.

"Oh thank goodness! With all of the parties and mayhem tonight you guys will probably beat the ambulance."

"Can you get out of a window?" Jade asks.

"He's got some sort of heavy metal screen on the windows. Dammit! I got to get out of here. If the Fire Department has to pull me out here I'll end up on the morning news as part of that Hallo-Weenies segment. Plus, I'll be all over social media looking like a doof."

"Look around, maybe you can find something to pry it open."

"He probably has a lever on the window screen so that he can escape if there's a fire. She should feel around for a tucked latch." Scott says.

"Scott says to feel around on the screen for release lever. Oh and we just pulled up outside."

Jade and Scott park a couple of doors down from the house.

"Scott I don't want to end up on someone's social media feed. Let me use your Halloween hockey mask."

"I have a better idea. Use that Myers mask in the bag on the back seat. I got too hot when I put it on so I was going to take it back to the store."

"Okay. Let's go get her."

Joe feels around the edges of the screen. Finally, she touches a handle at the bottom of the window frame and the screen pops opens. She opens the window. She looks down and sees a tall guy wearing a hockey mask standing next to a shorter person wearing a Mike Myers mask standing near the bushes below the window.

Scott whispers loudly, "I'm on the Pep Squad. I always catch the girl at the top of the pyramid. Jump down and I will catch you."

"No! That sounds crazy!" Joe says in a loud whisper.

They can hear can hear sirens approaching.

"The ambulance is coming Joe. You better jump down." Jade says.

"Don't worry, I only dropped one-person last year." Scott says.

"I'm not comforted by that." Joe whispers to them.

"Come on sis. We gotta go! Plus, it's frickin cold as balls out here." Jade says.

"Um balls are warm Jade." Scott says.

Jade tilts her head, gives him a scornful look under the Myers mask.

"Really Scott? She says before smacking him on the shoulder with her open hand.

Joe hears the sirens getting closer. She climbs onto to the window ledge, then shimmies down so the she can hang onto the ledge by her fingers.

She closes her eyes and let's go of the ledge. The bow in her hair snags on the sill and comes loose; dangling like a veil in her face.

Scott holds out his arms and catches her. In his exuberance over catching Joe he thrusts his arms in the air and yells, "*Woo-Hoo!*"

One of Dan's neighbors turns on their porch light. Joe, Jade and Scott walk quickly down the street to the car. They pull away and pass the ambulance and the police when they reach the end of Dan's street.

"I feel bad that I left Dan laying on the floor."

"Oh please! The paramedics will take care of that paranoid nutcase. Hey are you wearing Z-scars? I thought that you hated that horror stuff."

"I don't want to talk about it." Joe says.

Joe and Jade arrive home to find Jaxx and their mom pacing in the kitchen.

"What's wrong?" Jade asks.

"We can't find Julz!" Her mother says through tears.

"*What?*" Joe shouts.

"We've called the hospitals. The police won't do anything because she hasn't been missing long enough."

Their mom points to the small TV in the kitchen. "Thankfully we haven't seen anything about Julz on the local news either." Their mom says.

Jaxx continues calling her sister's phone, but there is no answer. Finally, her line picks up.

"Julz! Julz? Oh thank goodness you're ok. I was so worried. Julz? Say something." Jaxx says.

A man's voice is heard through the receiver.

"Hello. I have your sister."

"Oh my gosh! Are you a kidnapper?" Jaxx asks.

"Put him on speaker." Jade says.

"No! No! This is David Greene aka D.B. Greene. What I meant is that Julz wasn't feeling well so I brought her to my house. She's sleeping, but she seems fine. I'll bring her home as soon as she wakes up. I assure you she is safe with me, but give me the best number just in case I need to call you. You can reach me at 555-1738." David says.

"Okay, but please call if something happens to her health." Jaxx pleads.

"Absolutely! Will do." David says.

"Mom I think that she's ok." Jaxx says.

Her mother speaks through heavy tears, "You think? What do you mean by you think? I want to be certain that my baby is ok. I want to make sure that my baby is fine. I think we should Sumner."

"No Mom. We know how he handles things. Besides, she's not a baby. Maybe we need to ease up and let her be a grown up."

"I know that she's a grown up, but she's still my baby. My very fragile baby."

Jaxx continues to hold her sobbing mother. She also begins to cry. Jaxx reaches passed her mom and takes Joe's hand. Joe looks up at Jaxx.

"I know Mom. I had to force myself to pull back too. Maybe we need to stop worrying so much about her life and just let her live." Jaxx says.

"I know, but it's hard." Her mom says.

Joe nods at Jaxx as she accepts her oldest sister's words as both an apology and a promise.

All of the ladies hug, sob and rock.

Jaxx walks her mother upstairs to her bedroom. Joe and Jade remain in the kitchen.

"Wow this has been a crazy night huh?" Jade asks.

"Crazy doesn't begin to describe it." Joe says.

Both of them turn towards the TV when the news caster announces *"Breaking News!"*

"This is Reese Collins from station W.C.O.U. I'm coming to you live from the corners of West University Heights Drive and Dylan. It looks like there's been some wild Halloween hijinks tonight. The police and paramedics are being tight lipped about a call that brought them to the area. However, a young man showed us a recording of some shenanigans that he uploaded to social media tonight. Here's a clip.

The newscaster cuts to a grainy video of woman falling from a second story window of home. She falls into the arms of a person wearing a hockey mask who is standing next to a person in a Myers mask. The person in the hockey mask throws up his arms and yells "Woo-Hoo" after catching the person falling from the window.

The newscaster returns to the air.

"That's just a preview of what you'll see on this year's segment of Hallo-Weenies. Oh and if you have any information about fake Jason, Lady Mike Myers and whoever that is wearing the bride's veil thing, the police would like to speak to you about some activity that happened in this area. Catch the rest of the Halloween fun tomorrow morning on W.C.O.U's annual segment of *Hal-lo-Wee-nies. Sponsored by the makers of Eve's Helper.*"

"*Gee-zus!*" Joelle exclaims as she plants her face firmly into the palm of her left hand.

Jade reaches into the drawer and pulls out two spoons. She walks over to the freezer and grabs a tub of Mabel-Anne's Pumpkin, Pecan Caramel Crunch ice cream and then hands Joe a spoon.

Joe digs into the creamy goodness.

"Well at least you looked cute in your costume on TV." Jade says as she scoops out a spoonful of ice cream.

Joe replies, "Yep. Thanks."

The two sisters sit in the kitchen sighing aloud while eating ice cream.

Part Five

Julz awakens in a king sized bed with fancy linens. She panics with confusion when she looks around at the unfamiliar large bedroom that is far more luxurious than the simple above the garage apartment she lives in. She admires the beams in the cathedral ceiling. Luxurious suede drapes run from the ceiling to the floor. She walks over to a tall and wide window. The picturesque view of snowcapped mountains and ice frosted lake takes her breath away. She turns around and sees a note sitting on top of some black lady's active wear trimmed in pink laying on a cushion at the foot of the bed. She reads:

"Julz, please feel free to use the shower. I sent my friend out to pick up some fresh clothes, makeup, and lady toiletries. Come on out and have breakfast when you're ready. I'll be around the house." David

She walks into the full body shower with a rain-head spout. She rubs her hands across the natural black and silver streaks in the dark blue marble. She uses a fancy bar of orange blossom glycerin soap to lather up a soft wash cloth to scrub away the filth from the night before. The warm water feels good on her bruised skin. As she washes her body she finds strips of bandages stuck to her butt cheeks and the back of her thighs. She pulls one off and is amused and upset that someone stuck children's bandages to her bottom while she was unconscious. She dries off and moisturizes with orange blossom lotion. She gets dressed.

Meanwhile in the living room, David loudly discusses his displeasure about internet piracy with Youngblood; while his brother Ronnie prepares food in the kitchen.

"Are you telling me that it's legal for Grundel-Play to display my eBook for free without my permission? This is bull! What's the point of me trying to sell my work when some internet company can just give it away? Fair? What do you mean they said they are trying to be fair? Fair is one the worst four letter words in business. It usually means that the person

who it's being said to is about to get screwed. We need to sue them!"

"Many have tried and failed." Youngblood says.

"Oh this is serious B-S!" David shouts.

"Watch that BP and breathe. You don't want to bring on a health hiccup." Youngblood says.

"You're right. Let me calm down."

"The good news is that most people prefer to read a hard copy book. Plus, your audiobook sales are outstanding." Youngblood says.

"It's the principle of the thing man. No one should do what they want with my work without my permission." David says.

Ronnie looks up from chopping vegetables on the cutting board in the kitchen and notices that Julz has entered the room. He clears his throat. "Ah-hem! It looks like the bunny has awakened. Good morning snow bun-neee." He sings.

"Morning Julz. I hope that you're feeling better today." David says.

"*Morning*." Julz sings.

"This is my good friend and agent Youngblood."

Youngblood stands up and nods.

"I hope that you like the stuff I picked out for you." David says.

"Everything is very nice thank you." She says.

"The guy in the kitchen is my brother Ronnie." David says.

Ronnie waves hello. "I picked out the orange blossom soaps and feminine wash."

"Thank you that was very thoughtful. Now I'm orange blossom fresh from my rooter to my tooter." She says.

"Ha-ha-hah! You're welcome." Ronnie says with a smile.

"And thanks for patching me up with Super Duper Gyro Friends bandages." She says.

"Oddly the pharmacy was sold out of adult bandages. At least I got a chance to use my old military self-aid and buddy care training. Ha-ha!" David says.

Youngblood excuses himself and joins Ronnie in the kitchen.

"Sorry for interrupting you, but my phone died and I need to let my family know where I am." Julz says.

"Don't worry they know where you're at. Listen to the message your family left on my phone." David says before playing a message from her Mom and sister.

"Julz this is your Mom. Please call me because we're worried about you. On second thought don't call because you an adult and we trust you to do the right thing, but we're worried."

Jaxx interrupts her mom on the recording. "Listen horror writer, if anything happens to my sister, we'll cut off your little berries and press them in one of your books."

Her mother chimes in – "And that's with a butter knife too."

"We love you Julz!" Jade and Joe add in.

Julz slaps her forehead with the palm of her left hand. Her face flushes with embarrassment.

"Oh my God I am sooo sorry about that. They can be a little overprotective. I'll get my things and head out." She says.

"It snowed pretty heavy overnight. You can't get a PAT to travel through this much snow. Don't worry. They usually plow the roads around here by 1 pm. You might as well kick back and get something to eat."

"Where did you put the rest of my things? And how the heck did I get out of my costume?" Julz asks.

"Your costume is in the dryer. And Ronnie removed your clothes."

"Great! Now more people have seen my T and A." Julz blushes.

"Don't worry girl. Your T, A, and P are safe with me. I'm strictly into tall guys with money. Know your value girl.

Get with the ones who will upgrade your worth." Ronnie yells from the kitchen.

David walks over to a console, presses a button. A partition slides to cut off the kitchen from the living room and dining area.

"Man don't be like that. You know how nosey we are." Ronnie says.

"I put the bottle of meds that fell out of your pocket in a bag with your boots. Its sitting by the night stand."

"Oh okay. I'll go get it." Julz says.

"Wait a minute Julz. You were pretty sick last night. At one point you were having mild tremors. You'll probably get mad at me for getting in your business, but you were adamant about not going to the hospital so I contacted my doctor. I told him what was going on with you falling and slurring and he said that you were displaying the side effects of someone taking too high of a dose of that autoimmune system drug you're on. My doc said break the pills in half before taking your next dose. I know troops and vets with Gulf War Syndrome Lupus who use the same drug for the same kind of flare-uh..."

She interrupts David with a hint of annoyance in her voice; "You're right, I am mad that you got in my business, but last night you probably stopped me from becoming a human popsicle so thank you for that."

"If you ever want to talk about what you're…" David says.

She interrupts him again. "I don't want to talk about my past or any of my most embarrassing moments. I don't ever want to talk about any of this ridiculous mess!" Julz says as she chokes back tears.

She walks back into the bedroom. David joins the others in the kitchen.

"I pissed her off." He says.

"Nah, she's just mad at the whole messed up situation. People get a little funky when they're going through health crap remember?" Ronnie asks.

David drops his gaze to the floor. "Yeah, I remember." He says.

"Give her a minute. She'll be fine." Youngblood says.

"Look guys let's bring up the mood in here. Have a Mimosa." Ronnie says as he passes each of them a drink.

Julz speaks from the entryway to the kitchen, "Make mine a double."

"*Heck yeah!* Come on in." Ronnie says.

David looks at her and smiles. He finds her stubborn determination charming.

Part Six

A few weeks later at Wicked Ink & More Jaxx is prepping to install the organic fang implant for Sharnia. She starts to file the fangs, but notices that one of the fangs grew shorter than the other.

"*Shoot!*" She declares out loud.

She starts to file the longer fang down, but decides against it. She opts to angle it in a way that her client, Sharnia will not notice. Jaxx is a perfectionist who hates to do things halfway. She ponders the cost of inserting an imperfect vaginal fang implant or anger a $10,000 client at the holidays with news that they will have to regrow the implant from scratch. Jaxx opts to silently install the imperfect organic implant in Sharnia.

"Good morning Sharnia. Here's your fang implant." Jaxx shows the part to the client.

She installs the implant.

"Sharnia we're going to wheel you over to our recovery wing."

Sharnia listens in a light daze.

"Nurse Terra Fett will be your care giver. I will leave you with instructions for care. Remember, do not insert anything into the vaginal region or take baths for six weeks. I'll check on you tomorrow. I hate to leave you here over the holiday."

"Oh it's just another day to me."

"Well, I'll be on standby if there is an emergency. Have a good night."

"Same to you doctor."

*****

A heavy wooden door swings open into a large shed. Subdued dusk light barely illuminates a shirtless man sitting in the middle of the shed slumped over in a chair with a dirty cloth sack covering his head. The noise of footsteps on the concrete floor stir the man in the chair. The man in the chair shouts towards the sound of the footsteps.

"I don't know who you are, but you got the wrong guy!"

The man in the chair can hear the sounds of heavy truck engines and loud swishing sounds of air brakes on a semi-truck. The loud truck noises grow softer as he hears the machines move further away. In the quiet the sound of someone loudly turning pages fills the room, but the page turner takes long pauses between page turns as if reading. He hears someone slam something on a surface to his right. His heart sinks when he hears a man with a familiar Cajun accent speak.

"Excuse the noise. Construction deadlines have us workin' into the late hours of the night. Now I'm gone make this quick 'cause I have to get to a dinner affair. Are you Stephen Raymond Bowe - aka Stevie Ray - aka Sticky Bowe; arrested twenty-three times for larceny, eight times for strong arm robbery, three times for battering women and one arrest for public intoxication while engaging in lascivious acts in a koi pond? I'm not sure what kind of sick thangs you were doing with big ole goldfish; and frankly I don't want to know. At any rate, is the aforementioned your work?"

"Nawl. That ain't me." The man in the chair says.

"That ain't you huh?"

"Nawl man I'm not familiar with that person so basically that ain't me."

Sumner sits on the edge of a desk cleaning his nails with a large hunting knife with the words Trouble-Sum

engraved into the handle.

Someone suddenly snatches the cloth sack off of the head of the man sitting in the chair. Now the man in the chair can match the accent to the face of the guy from the tattoo shop. He also sees two burly men standing on each side of the man from the tatt shop.

Sumner walks over and points his large hunting knife towards the neck of the robber.

"You keep saying that you ain't the one, but why is it that you have a tattoo on your neck that says Sticky B. and a tatt on your shoulder that says Stevie-Get-Some-Ray?"

"Just a coincidence. I don't know what you're talking about." The robber says.

"Stick-up Man, on top of everything else you gone sit here and insult me by lying to my face or should I call you Stevie-no-nose?" Sumner says as he points his knife towards the middle of the robber's face.

"Ok-okay I'm sorry about trying to stick-up that tattoo place. I wasn't going to hurt your family."

"Oh, but you did hurt my fam-ley Stick-up Man. Now they don't feel safe and protected no-mo."

"After what them heffas did to me by beating me up like that, the broads are lucky that I didn't come back for a little pay back."

"Well you still sound a little salty; bad mouthing my fam-ley like that."

"Oh, you don't have to worry about me getting revenge. I swear that I'll clean up my life and leave town."

Sumner sits down on the edge of the desk again.

"I'm sure that you've offered to clean up your life over a dozen times to over a dozen judges, but you've never cleaned up your life or left town. Some time ago, I remember that there was this old gator that used to leave the swamp to find somebody's swimming pool to wade in every summer. Fish and Game Officers would go swoop him up every year and take him back to the swamp. This move the gator game went on for years. One year one of the Game Officers found that old gator sunning himself in his pool while flossing his teeth with his dog's leash.

You would've thought that the Officer would've put that nuisance gator down right then and there, but he took that critter back to its home in the swamp.

That old gator never bothered anyone ever again. Do you know what the moral of the story is?"

"It seems like it would be about forgiveness for a troublesome, yet harmless creature and in the end helping the troubled one find their way home."

"Nope. The moral of the story is that no matter how much grace you give to a nuisance predatory creature, they'll eventually get around to preying on you and yours so it's best to send that predator permanently home."

Sumner moves swiftly to personally send the robber permanently home by way of the sharp edge of his trusty blade called Trouble-Sum.

"Nobody messes with my people!" Sumner whispers.

*****

The Havreaux's two story home is brightly lit with holiday decorations both inside and out. Julz dances around her mother's house setting the table and touching up little details for her family's Annual Happy Holidays dinner party.

"Shake that booty to the right and place a napkin. Move that booty to the left and place a napkin." Julz is downright ecstatic that she has had fewer health issues ever since she had her medication adjusted. Except for several bouts of her buttocks and upper legs going numb, she hasn't tumbled to the ground in a few weeks. She rotates her booty around and around then jiggles it as she adjusts the small poinsettia table settings.

Her mother walks into the dining room and catches Julz dancing to one of the latest pop tunes. Jade and Joe catch Connie doing some old school 1970s dance moves.

"Go Mom. Go Mom. Go-go go Mom." Jade says.

"Go Julz! Go Jade! Go-Joe! Now go to the kitchen and help your sister finish the hors d' oeuvres. We only have a couple of hours before the guests arrive." Connie says.

"Okay. Mom how many people are coming again?" Julz asks.

"Eight. Wait, um twelve. I almost forgot that Barbara is bringing her cousins that recently moved to town. So no more than twelve." Connie says.

"Plus us? That's fifteen hungry mouths to feed. Do you think that we have enough food?" Julz asks.

"Several people are bringing dishes like they did last year." Connie says.

"Oh goody, another year of pumpkin and cranberry side dishes." Julz rolls her eyes then booty bops her way into the kitchen.

She sees her sister standing at the long island making a holiday salad.

"Hey Jaxx. How'd it go with the spider lady?" Julz booty bops over to sink and washes her hands.

Jade walks into the kitchen.

"The procedure went as smooth as silk. No pun intended."

"I'm not surprised by much in this business, but what in the free nation of frosted bees man?"

"I know right? I try to ignore the edgy stuff too, but this one falls in the what in the weird and unusual category." Jaxx says.

"For sure." Julz says.

"Hey, I heard Mom say that she wants you to make up a tray of those smoked salmon cream cheese rolls. The cucumbers are over there. I love those things." Jaxx says.

"Ooo I do too, but I always forget an ingredient when I make them." Jade says.

"Come over here little Sis and I'll show you how to make them. You just blend cream cheese with fresh dill, a little basil, a splash of lemon and a pinch of ground cayenne in a bowl. Cut a four-inch-long thin piece of smoked salmon. Spread a thin layer of the cream filling on the salmon. Roll it into a log. Now slice it like bread. Put the pieces on top of each slice of cucumber. Top with a pinch of fresh dill and viola'! You have salty, creamy crunchy deliciousness."

Joe walks into the kitchen and pops one of the salmon rolls in her mouth.

Joe speaks with food in her mouth.

"I bet that I could add a drop of green food coloring for a St Patty's Day party too."

"Yeah, good idea." Jaxx says.

"Thanks Julz! Next you'll have to show me how to cook a turkey." Jade says.

"You'll cook it on low at 325 degrees and slow for several hours depending on the size; but always remember to?"

Jaxx, Jade, Joe and Julz speak in unison. "Always take the giblet bag out of the bird's butt!" They all laugh.

"Haha! I remember that part from Aunt Marie's Thanksgiving disaster." Jade laughs.

"Yep. Season it inside and out, cover it with foil and baste it every 30 minutes until its done."

Julz booty bops her way over to the fridge, grabs more fresh dill, and then booty bops to the other end of the island. She does a gyrating booty bop over to the knife drawer and gyrates back to the island.

Jaxx stops tossing salad ingredients into a bowl when her sister's odd booty jerking dance catches her attention.

"Um Julz, you might want to find another way to loosen up that numb butt of yours. You're starting to look like a twerker with hemorrhoids." Jaxx says.

Julz stops moving. "Oh crap! Do I? I have to do something about my numb butt problem."

"How 'bout something a little subtler like clenching your butt cheeks? Besides, you can't shake your booty like that while we're sitting at the dinner table anyway."

"Good point."

Ring Dong! Connie opens the door. Sumner is standing there holding a large pot with a silver bowl sitting on top of it.

"Happy Holidays mon cher!" Sumner leans in and gives her a kiss on the cheek.

"What's with this Happy Holidays stuff?"

"I like to cover all em Sis."

"Haha! What cha got in the pots Sum?"

"Oh just my famous seafood gumbo, my famous Beignets (ben-yays) and fradd gator bites. I even brought three kinds of dipping sauce. Go on Sis, reach in dair and get you a taste of gator."

Connie grabs a nugget of fried alligator. She closes her eyes as she savors it. She smiles as the scrumptious spices remind her of the Bayou.

"Sumner you have really out done yourself. Man I haven't had these in years. These were Jim's favorites."

"Yes they were. Lawd rest my brother's soul."

Connie leans in to whisper to Sumner.

"I heard that the gunman who threatened the girls is back on the streets. I'm really worried that we're gonna have a problem with him coming back for some payback after the beat down they gave him."

"On the bones of my brother you know I'll always watch over y'all. That robber is one problem that ain't gone bother nobody no mo. Oh and I'm keeping my eyes on that writer fella too."

Without blinking she looks him straight in the eyes before responding, "Good and good." She tosses him a devilish smile.

Ring Dong!

"Sumner go on and put your food over there on the buffet. I have to get the door."

Connie welcomes answers the door.

"*Thomasina!* Hey lady it's been a long time! Thanks for coming."

"Here Connie; I brought you a sweet potato pie with buttered pecan garnish."

"Thank you! Girl you shouldn't temp me with one of my favorite pies. My post holidays diet will need some supernatural help." She laughs.

"This is my husband William and my youngest son Josh." Thomasina says.

"Please to meet you. Where can I put our coats?" William asks.

"On the rack in the back room." Connie says

"Josh is an Ophthalmologist at Saint Grace Hospital. He also stars in commercials for the dog shelter." Thomasina says.

"Oh my! A soon to be doctor and animal savior. You really are exceptional." Connie says.

"I'm just doing what I can to help out. Ma'am, do you have somewhere that I can put mom's pumpkin salad on ice?" He asks.

"Why don't you go into the kitchen and ask my daughter Julz for ice. Oh wait, Julz is standing over there by the dinner table. She'll be happy to help you with this." Connie says.

"Um Julz? Hi! Your mom said that you can help me put this salad on ice." Josh says.

"Sure follow me. You look familiar. I swear that I've seen you somewhere before." She says.

"If you've ever had any serious eye problems you may have seen me around the hospital."

"Nah, I swear it's from somewhere else." Julz says as they enter the kitchen.

Jaxx stops fiddling with the hors d'oeuvres when she recognizes Josh.

"Haaay! It's the doctor and dog-man guy from that Save the Shelter commercial."

"Guilty as charged. I love helping out at the shelter, but I hated doing the commercial. Too much sitting gives me numb butt." Josh says.

"Well aren't you perfect. It appears that you and Julz have a lot in common." Jaxx says.

Julz picks up a tray of hors d' oeuvres.

"Let me help you with that. Is this smoked salmon? I love these!" Josh picks up the tray. He and Julz take it to the buffet table.

"Thanks for the help. Oh I think that I have something in my left eye." Julz says.

Josh pulls out a tiny black flashlight from his pocket. "Let me take a look at it. Hold your head back."

The doorbell rings. Connie opens the door. "Welcom…" She's surprised to see the guests at the door.

"Hi Connie. These are my cousins Ronnie and David, and his agent Youngblood." Barbara says.

"Happy Holidays Mrs. Havreaux. Hide all of the sharp knives because the scary horror writer is here. Haha!" David laughs nervously.

"And butter the knives too." Ronnie whispers.

Connie smiles through pursed lips.

"Well look at you, a horror writer and a comedian too. Listen, things went down pretty screwy a few weeks ago, but thanks again for helping Julz." Connie says with a little attitude.

"It was no problem at all." David says.

"Now go grab something to eat. Julz is over." She says

"I see her. *Haaayy Snow Bun-nee!*" Ronnie yells across the room.

For four weeks Julz has remained anonymous in the face of jokes, weak memes and general shade being thrown on social media about an unidentified drunk bunny on Halloween. Were it not for social media she would have successfully avoided anything that reminds her of that night; this is until now.

Julz is so startled by a familiar voice screaming a reminder of one of the most embarrassing moments of her life that when she whips her head towards the sound, she accidently rams her left eyeball into the mini flashlight that Josh is holding.

"*What the fudge!*" Julz screams as she covers her eye.

Connie runs over to help her daughter. "Oh no! Julz are you okay?" Connie says.

"Uhn-uhn-uhn! They need to wrap that girl's head in bubble wrap or Styrofoam or maybe just strap a pillow to her so that she can stop hurting herself. Lord fix it!" Ronnie snaps. David elbows Ronnie in the side.

Everyone sits down to dinner. At one end of the table Connie sits with her older friends. In the middle area Jaxx, Joe and Jade play hosts to a few guests, and at the other end Julz plays hostess to David and his crew. David sits directly across from Julz; Youngblood on his left and his brother Ronnie on his right. Josh sits to the left of Julz. The guests are cheerfully eating, drinking, and laughing.

Julz is feeling uncomfortable about sitting in front of the guy who she has experienced two shameful public incidents with. She eats in silence with her eyes cast down to her plate.

David repeatedly glances at her from across the table. He doesn't know why, but he is feeling some type of way towards the woman before him.

Josh notices David's fascination with Julz. He shoots David a dirty look before speaking.

"Julz are you chasing the lights this year?"

"I'm thinking about it. I registered to get the text alert, but I'm on the fence. How about you?"

"I'm going to do it. Catching a sight of those dancing lights doesn't come around every day. My friends and I dressing up in superhero costumes. I'm a player; cosplayer that is. I'd be happy if you joined me Julz." Josh says.

"Like I said I'm still thinking about it."

Julz feels the numbing sensation in her buttocks growing worse so she tries clenching her butt cheeks for relief. With each booty clench her upper body rises in her chair and upon unclenching her upper body lowers into her seat. She slowly bobs up and down in her seat like a human fishing bob dancing in the sea. A few guests begin to stare at her. Josh starts bobbing up and down in his seat too.

Ronnie breaks the silence. "Okay I'll ask. Are you two doing some sort of chair yoga?"

Josh responds as he continues to bob in his chair, "Numb butt."

Jules throws her head back and laughs loud. Other guests laugh too.

David is not amused. He takes a big gulp of red wine before speaking to Josh,

"Don't you play a doctor in TV commercials?"

"No I'm a doctor in real life, but I'm featured in commercials. I'm not big on playing pretend." Josh shoots David a menacing look.

David takes the comment as a personal swipe at him for being a fiction writer. He returns the glare at the doctor.

Ronnie bumps David's leg under table and then whispers in his ear.

"Take a breath bro."

David whispers through clenched teeth,

"I'm fine."

"But you're picking your teeth with your steak knife and people look concerned."

Ronnie smiles and nods at the other guests staring at his brother.

"Oh." David replies before putting down the knife.

Julz turns to Josh.

"Tell us a crazy doctor story Josh."

"Okay, here's one. A man walks in and complains that he gets grit in his eye every time he drives to the eye doctor. The doctor asks what he does differently on the drive that he doesn't do at home…"

The combination of a bad night's sleep and the doctor droning on and on prompts David to nod off, but he quickly catches himself and jerks his body awake; kicking Julz under the table in the process. Julz shoots David a mean look. David nods off again, but jerks awake before he kicks Jules again. This time Jules squints her eyes in anger at him before she draws her foot back and kicks David very hard in his ankle. David yells "Ow!" He then accidently knocks over his wine glass; spilling red wine into his lap. He jumps up from the table. David uses his napkin to try to soak up the wine from his shirt and pants.

All of the guests focus their attention on the activity at the other end of the table. Connie interrupts the scene.

"Oh it looks like we have a spill. Julz take David to the laundry and use the stain wand thing on him before that wine sets in."

"Don't worry about it. Just point me to it and I'll take care of it." David says.

Julz gets up from the table. "Oh come on!" Julz grumbles at David.

Julz searches around the laundry room, but she only finds an empty tube of stain remover. "I have some more at my place. Follow me." She says.

They walk outside towards a three car garage. David heads towards the stairs leading up to her apartment. She stops him and opens the door to the smaller entryway of the garage. "I no longer use the stairs. My dad had an elevator installed in this part of the garage."

They step off of the elevator into her apartment.

"Very nice! It's a lot more spacious than I imagined. I dig the open kitchen, dining and living room style too." David says.

"Thanks. It's not bad for an upgraded mother-in-law's suite."

He notices her book collection.

"I see that you're an avid reader."

He walks over to a book shelf.

"Scratch that. These are physics books. You working on becoming a scientist?"

"I was, but life got in the way. I guess I'm an eclectic mix of a woman who wanted to a be scientist who ended up being a tattoo artist huh?"

"Not really. I'm an engineer who became a horror writer. Destiny works in eclectic ways."

"So true. Take your shirt and pants off so that I can help you with that stain." She says.

"Oh you don't have to do that. I can scrub it out." He says.

"It's the least I can do after you helped me." Julz says.

David starts to unbutton his shirt. He bares his chiseled chest and Julz quickly turns her head.

"Don't tell me you're shy. You look at shirtless men all of the time at your tattoo place."

Julz fusses with the cap on the tube of stain remover.

"The clients are already undressed when I see them. It's a lot more clinical. It's kind of weird having a guy undress in my house. Cover up with that throw on the sofa." She averts her eyes to the counter.

David pulls off his shirt. "Just do the shirt. I'll do my pants." He says.

"Okay I'll work on your shirt in the laundry room. You can work on your pants in the kitchen. Bring them to my laundry room in the back when you're ready and I'll toss your clothes in the dryer."

"Thanks, but there's no need to go out of your way." He says.

"Like I said, I owe you." She says.

"Hey it's pretty chilly in here." He says.

"I'll turn on the fireplace." Julz says.

David rushes over to the fireplace and warms his hands in the heat.

"Would you like something to drink? I have cognac and ale." She says

"Cognac, but please have a holiday toast with me."

"Okay."

She pours their drinks and then hands David a snifter of cognac.

"Happy Holidays! He says.

They clink glasses. He notices a picture sitting on the mantel over the fireplace of a middle aged man wearing a blue military sports coat. David nods towards the picture.

"Is that your dad?"

"Yes, it is."

"Ah yes, an Air Force man. Will he be joining the party?"

"No. He passed on a few years ago. It was a traffic accident."

"I'm sorry to hear that."

   Her phone rings. She sits her glass down on the coffee table in the living room. It's my mother. Yes, Mom? Oh yeah, you are out of stain remover so I brought him up here. Uhn-huh – Uhn-huh. Why are you yelling?" Julz turns towards David and then nods and silently mouths to him that she'll be in the backroom.

"Yes mother." She continues speaking on the phone.

David acknowledges with an up and down head nod and a smile.

Julz continues to speak to her mother as she walks to a back room. "Mother stop worrying. Everything is fine." She goes into a room and then closes the door.

David receives a text from his brother.

"Dr. Douche heading your way."

David sends a typed reply: "Thanks. It'll probably take an hour before my clothes are ready."

"Roger that."

He hears a light knocking at the front door and a low voice.

"Julz? It's Josh. Your mother sent me to check on you." He whispers loudly.

David sits his drink down on the coffee table. He drapes the sofa-throw over his left shoulder and secures it around his waist with one hand before opening the door.

"May I help you doctor?"

"Mrs. Havreaux asked me to see if Julz needed anything." The doctor says.

"Julz is fine, but she's unavailable at the moment. As you can see we just sat down to have drinks by the fire."

David nods to the two classes of cognac on the coffee table.

"I'll tell her that you stopped by. Oh and Doctor, I may write about pretend things, but this is how I roll in real life – *playa*! Happy Thanksgiving!" David closes the door.

Julz returns to the living room.

"I just remembered that I have these active wear sets in box. We're giving them away over the holidays to promote the shop. I think these should fit you. I'll leave them on the sofa. You can change in the guest bathroom over there."

"Thanks." He says.

She shivers and rubs her cold shoulders.

"You're right David. It's flippin freezing in here! It feels like I left the windows and the door open."

He adjusts his blanket as he responds. "I know right? Burrrrr! Let's warm up by the fireplace."

Julz sees part of a familiar tattoo on his upper back.

"Yes, let's do that Mr. Smith." She says sternly.

"Oh – um, about that." David says.

"What have you been doing, *stalking me*?" She asks.

"No, I needed to get my tatt fixed, but after the incident at my book signing, I stopped by your shop to apologize in person. Unfortunately, you showed up as a robot. What's up with that robot thing anyway? And why haven't you scheduled me yet?" He asks.

"It's my legs okay. Sometimes they just don't work right. Lately, they've been acting up more than usual. You don't know what it's like for me. You couldn't possibly understand my monsters with your big beautiful house, perfect health, perfect bod-..." She stops talking when David drops the blanket he's wearing to the floor.

He stands there in silence facing her, wearing nothing but his white boxer briefs. Julz can now see that the same patchy leathery scars that she saw on his lower back in the tattoo shop, partially cover the left side of his perfectly chiseled abs. The scars run down his lower left side and what's left of his entire left leg. She sees that the width of his leg below his thigh is two thirds the size of what it should be for a man with the build of a fit baseball player who is almost six feet tall.

"David I'm so sorry. Sometimes I just…"

He interrupts her. "Don't worry, you didn't know. I may not be able to understand what you're going through, but I assure you that I know a lot about where you've been. I get how hard it is when your body doesn't work the way that you want it to, but you keep going anyway. Even when I'm exhausted from lack of sleep because I've been fighting war monsters in my head all night, I tell myself to keep going. Even when I'm so tired that I can't stay awake while I'm having Thanksgiving dinner while sitting across from a very beautiful woman, I still tell myself that I got to keep going. No, Julz I may not understand all of your struggles, but I am *certainly* not afraid of *your* monsters."

She flashes a diminished smile. "You-you think that I'm beautiful?" She asks.

David blushes.

"I think that you're frickin hot!" He says.

He picks up the blanket. "Now let me cover up before my scars give you another barfing attack."

She walks over to him and looks into his eyes with understanding. She gently tugs at the blanket.

"I think you're beautiful too." She says.

He quivers as she lightly rubs her right hand over the scars covering the muscles on his abdomen. She likes how his scars feel rough and soft at the same time; just like soft kid leather painted over hard muscles.

She can feel his breathing quicken as she slowly moves her hand up his left side to his chest; exploring every inch of his skin along the way. She glides her hand along his body up to the side of his face. He closes his eyes as she runs her fingers through his hair. Her body quivers as she feels his breath and lips on the palm of her hand. He inhales and exhales deep while tenderly kissing the inside of her wrist.

Tweep-tweep-tweep! Tweep, tweep, tweep.

Julz slides her hands away from David, then answers her phone.

"That's Jaxx's code for Mom's coming. You need to put something on A-S-A-P!"

"Julz, let's get to know each other. How about you personally work on my tatt and we'll talk? I promise I will keep my hands to myself."

She stands silent. She can hear her mother walking on her stairs.

"Say yes." He says.

She can hear her mother getting closer.

Her mother shouts from the staircase, "*Geez Julz you need to get someone over here to shovel your walkway and stairs. This place is a death trap!*"

"Your mom is about to catch me half naked in your house by a cozy fire. What's your answer?"

"Okay, okay - yes. Put these clothes on right now! Butter knife, berries in your book remember?" She says through clenched teeth.

"Roger that!" He grabs the clothes and runs into the bathroom.

Julz opens her door. "Hey Mom what's going on?"

"I found my stain remover. This brand will work better than the one that you have." She says.

David comes out of the bathroom wearing black active wear with the Wicked Sisters Ink & More logo on the shirt."

"Hello Mrs. Havreaux. Sorry about the mess at dinner." David says.

"No worries. I'll help Julz clean up your clothes. It will be fine for you to rejoin the party in that outfit. Julz and I will get this done pretty quick."

David leaves the house.

Her mother stands at the kitchen sink treating the stains on David's pants.

"Sooo, it looked like you and the doctor were getting along well. He seems like a perfect fit for you honey."

"He's cute and very nice, but you know how it is Mom, he just doesn't have the allure of those magic beans."

Her mom glances over at two drink glasses sitting on Julz's coffee table.

"Hmm - I see." Her mother says.

Part Seven

Two days later Julz and David begin their ink session. He lays on his stomach while Julz prepares to work on the tatt on his back.

"Have you decided what design you want on your left side yet?" She asks.

"Not yet. I want something, but I still haven't found a design that moves me yet."

"Hmm?"

"Tell me something about you Julz. How did you get into this line of work?"

"As kids my sister and I used to try to outdo each other in everything art related. It didn't matter if it was kiddie clay sculptures or cookie decorating, we competed against each. Bowman's BBQ held a contest to design a giant piece of art to be a back drop for their stage area. The prize was $1000. Jaxx and I teamed up and created this two sided, three paneled art piece that glows in the dark. We won. After that guys asked us to design their tatts, but the local guy couldn't quite replicate our artwork. They used to call us the wicked inking sisters. Eventually we went through formal training and became certified tattoo artists and three years ago Wicked Sisters Ink & More was born."

"Wow! I saw that art piece. It's awesome! You ladies are very talented. I can't believe that the thing still glows in the dark. Have you had Bowman's white sweet potato fries? They are sooo goowood! Ohhhh!"

"You're a little too excited about those fries David. Um do you need a moment alone?"

"Ha-ha! No, but that spice blend on those fries though. Num-num-yum!"

"David I was wondering about – um-how do I ask?"

"What about my leg?"

"Yes, but I don't want to make you feel…"

"I'm cool with talking about it, but the details are pretty intense. I don't know if you can handle it."

"I can take it." She says excitedly. "Please tell me your story." She says.

"I was a Captain in the Air Force when it happened. I was on one of two helicopters on a night training mission in the desert. We were on a training exercise to tighten up our proficiency to rescue people at night in rugged desert terrain. We were using night vision goggles on a flight just before 1am.

Sometimes I'm the co-pilot, but on that day my buddy Youngblood took the seat instead. I sat close by. Everything was going fine until something went wrong with the other copter. It clipped us just before it crashed. It seemed like everything was moving in slow motion. I could even hear the fhutt-fhutt-fhutt-fhutt-fhutt of the helicopter's rotary blades slowing down. When our copter began to drop from the sky, I could feel the tugging of my stomach sinking as my body floated like I was on a floor drop ride at a fair, but this was no amusement ride.

Most of the violence happened pretty fast. My pilot was killed instantly. Loud sounds of huge metal pieces slamming and scraping against metal rang out all around us. Suddenly the back of the copter sheared off and exploded; killing everyone in the rear in a fire, but they didn't go right away because I could hear them screaming. I can still hear them screaming. My heart aches that I could not reach them; that I could not help them.

Somehow my seat harness came loose. During the rocking and rolling I was able to grab part of a seat to stop myself from sliding out of the open back end and into raging flames.

It was hard to maintain my grip because the seat I was holding onto was wet and slippery from a crewman's blood. I was tossed again, but I lost my grip and slid on my back towards the front. Just as I slid forward, the right side of Youngblood's seat broke loose and lifted off of the floor. As soon as my left leg slid under the seat, the chair rocked back into place and then chomped down hard on my leg like a vice; pinning me under the seat and against the wall.

Youngblood was unconscious. I kept screaming his name and kicking the back of his seat trying to wake him up so that I could break free, but it didn't help. That's when the fire started under the instrument panel in the cockpit. I watched the pilot's body go up like a torch. Quickly Youngblood and I were on fire. The flames traveled around my leg, but thankfully missed my boyz downstairs; otherwise I would've become a giant Ken doll. Oh the pain though. The pain from the fire and the seat squeezing my left leg was sooo intense! I thought that I was going to die.

Finally, my stomping on the back of Youngblood's seat awakened him. He woke up with his left side on fire too. He got up and lifted the seat off of me and pulled me out of the copter. That's all I remember. He said that I saved his life, but he actually saved mine.

As you can see, the doctors were able to save my leg. I thought was going to become part cyborg, but now I'm roasted turkey leg man instead.

It took years before I could listen to the sound of meat frying without it messing with my head.

Anyway, now I write about monsters. I used to write about them so that I could slay them, but I grew to love them instead. Funny how that worked out." He lowers his gaze and smiles to himself.

Julz intensely listens to David's story. She can see the entire scene playing in her like a clip from a movie. She can remember her hands touching pat of the story of his body. She feels her stomach and her heart stirring. A world of emotions flow through her. The feelings seemed confusing like joy and pain fighting with each other, but her soul knows what it was. It is the first time that the frost shield of her heart melted away. It's the first time that her heart is exposed to the welcoming heart of another. In this moment she finds herself falling in love with the brave wounded warrior laying before her. Two tears roll down her cheek and drip onto David's back.

"Hey something wet hit my back. I knew that I shouldn't tell you that sad story. Please don't cry."

"I'm not crying. It was drool." She sniffs as she silently wipes away more tears with her forearm.

"Drool? Really?" He hears what sounds like her trying to cry silently.

"Well that isn't very sanitary is it?"

"Don't worry, it missed your tatt." She uses a sani-cloth to wipe up the tears."

"Now I'll have infected with boils growing out of my tatt that will turn into eyes."

"Eyes?" She asks with a confused smile.

"Yes eyes. I'll be turning into a creature with eyes growing out of my back due to a liquid agent spilled by a mad ink doctor."

She starts laughing through her tears. "Hahaha! So that's how a horror writer's mind works huh? Your creature creation needs a little work though."

He smiles that he is able to make her laugh through her sadness. "Okay ink doctor, how would you write it?"

"Well I'd get rid of the eyes because they wouldn't be very functional."

"Oh?" He says.

"No. There should be monster arms with claws growing out of your back with a mind of their own."

"That's twisted. I love it! Go on." He says.

They joke around and laugh while she works.

"Hey I have an idea for your left arm and leg. Let's create a steampunk cyborg tatt down your entire left side. It will look like you're a cyborg that's been through a battle. You'll look like a half bad-azz cyborg warrior that doesn't look shiny and new."

"I really like that idea!"

"I can create a temporary tatt that we'll apply to your side so that you can see what it will look like when it's done. All of my sisters will have to help with this so that we can keep your overall recovery time low."

"Good deal. Let's rock!" He says.

Part Eight

Julz works on the cyborg design for two days in her home studio. She virtually sends the design to the team at Wicked Sisters Ink & More.

David Greene arrives at the tattoo shop first thing in the morning when the doors open. Jaxx, Jade, Joe and Terra put on short sleeve hospital scrubs, cloth cap and a mask around their necks. They stand at a large sink using hospital grade soap to scrub their forearms, hands and under their finger nails. Once they're all scrubbed up, the ladies put on rubber gloves. Jaxx insists on following appropriate infection control protocols especially for large human canvas jobs.

Terra enters the room where David is waiting.

"Good morning Mr. Greene. I'm going to prep you for your tattoo. Here's a little water and a pill Dr. Havreaux prescribed to help you through the procedure."

David takes the pill. He holds a towel over his private parts while Terra creates a half toga out of a sheet and then tapes the edges to the right side of his body. She makes a pocket under the half toga so that David can easily insert and remove his member if he has to go to the restroom. She applies numbing agent to the left side of his body from the crook of his neck, under his arm, half of his torso, over his buttock and all the way down his leg to the top of his foot. She applies the temporary design to the left side of his body.

Jaxx, Jade and Joe enter the room where David is prepped. Although Julz briefed them about David's condition they are psychologically taken aback at the sight of his extensive injuries.

"Morning David." They all sing out.

"Wow! Look at you guys all dressed out in hospital gear. Am I getting a tattoo or having something important removed? Hahaha."

Jaxx speaks for the crew. "We're all medically trained ink masters. We only gear up for the big jobs. Yours is a really big job. Here's how things will proceed.

Terra brings up David's tattoo design on a wall that converts into a video screen. The design is broken into two 3-dimensional images positioned side by side. The first image shows a slowly rotating pic of the cyborg design on the front and back of his torso. The second one shows the front and back of his leg design.

David barely listens to the briefing. The pill that he took is making him feel like he's lightly floating above the floor. He tries to look interested in what's being said, but he really doesn't care.

Jaxx continues. "We'll have you lie on your back while we work on the front design. Next we'll have you partially lay on the table while Joe does your back and I do your buttock and back of your leg. Since three of us will work on you at the same time, the total application time will be cut down to about seven hours. We'll take breaks as needed. Oh and let me know if you need something stronger for the pain and I'll give you something. Also, Julz was up pretty late working so she said she'll stop by later to check on you. Any questions?"

"No. Let's rock!" He says.

"Abigail, play random dance music. Dance 1, 5 repeat." Jade commands.

"Dance 1, 5 repeat?" David asks.

"Oh you'll see." Joe says

The little robot dog allows music to flow through the speakers imbedded in its sides. Abigail's head, shoulders and hind parts sway to the beat of the music on the first song and every fifth song that plays thereafter. On some songs the robot dog's wheels extend on thick silver cables to mimic human arms dancing in the wind. Julz programmed Abigail's music trick to amuse and relax clients during long ink sessions.

David watches the robot for a few seconds during the first song before laying down on the table.

"Haha! Cute." He laughs.

The sisters go to work on David. After several hours and a few breaks, the crew decides to take a break at the four-hour mark. As David starts to rise from the table a piece of tape comes loose allowing the toga to slip revealing his private parts to the ladies. David blushes as he quickly covers himself.

"Sorry about the slippage ladies."

He swiftly walks to the restroom.

The sisters race to the front desk where Daisy and Terra are standing. Jaxx, Jade and Joe stand at the desk wide eyed with weird smiling smirks on their faces.

"You guys look like my cat after he's done something naughty. Now dish!" Daisy says.

"I can't violate doctor patient confidentiality." Jaxx says.

"You all must've seen his tool. Based on how wide your eyes are it must be something else." Daisy says.

"I didn't see it. Was it comparable to Reindeer, Kielbasa or Polish sausage?" Terra asks.

With her eyes still open extremely wide Joe spouts, "Polish."

"Whaaad?" Terra says.

Just then David exits the restroom. The ladies tilt their heads as they watch him walk back to the tattoo application room.

"Happy Holidays Julz Havreaux!" Daisy says.

"Speaking of food, we should be done in about three hours. Let's order something from the M.A.T. (Meal Automated Transport) at the food mall. That way we can get anything that we want." Jade says.

"Good idea. I have a taste for old school smothered steak with gravy." Joe says.

"I want a lobster roll with carrot fries." Jade says.

"Hey is that place fully automated yet?" Jaxx asks.

"Almost. The owner is fighting a lot of labor protests in court, but automation is inevitable." Terra says.

"I shudder to think of what will happen to our jobs if ink master bots are invented." Jade says.

Jaxx scrunches her face and rapidly shakes her head at the horrid idea.

"I know right?" Jaxx says in agreement.

Daisy pulls up the menu app on a tablet. One by one they touch the option that they want. Jaxx asks David what he wants and she puts in his order. She even orders something for Julz. The bill is charged to their account and the order is scheduled for delivery.

"Well, back to work." Jaxx says.

The sisters continue working on David's half body tattoo. Three hours later the tattoo is done. See through bandages are applied to his new tatt.

"Alright David, we're done. How do you feel?" Jaxx asks.

"I'm a little sore, but I'm good. I'm also starving."

"Put on the light sweats that we laid out for you and meet us in the room next door for the food." Jaxx says.

"Okay." He says.

They all sit down to eat. Jaxx notices that Julz isn't there.

"Anyone heard from Julz?" Jaxx asks.

"I didn't receive any calls the front desk." Daisy says.

"We left our phones in the washroom. I'll call her to see what's up." Jaxx says.

"Tell her to come on or I'm going to eat her food. Haha!" David laughs.

Jaxx calls Julz, but receives no answer. She checks messages. A few minutes later Jaxx rushes back to the room looking and sounding panicked.

"I received a message from PAT Management that Julz was rushed to the hospital." Jaxx says.

The other sisters check their phones and sure enough the same message was sent to all emergency contacts listed on the chip in Julz's emergency bracelet.

"*Oh my God!*" Terra yells.

"I'm calling Mom." Jaxx says.

"I can fit everyone in my SUV. I'll drive us there." David says.

They lock up the ink shop. Everyone piles into David's vehicle then heads to the hospital. When they arrive at Flagstaff Medical, they see Connie Havreaux pacing alone in a waiting area.

"Mom what happened? Where's Julz?" Jade asks.

"A doctor told me that a PAT called for help after Julz went into distress and fell. Apparently she hit her head during the fall. They're working on her. That's all I was told. I don't know what condition she's in. Whether she's conscious or anything." Connie says through tears.

Jaxx puts her arms around her mother's shoulders.

"I have admitting privileges here. I'll snoop around to see what's going on."

"Okay baby." Her mother says.

Almost a half hour later Jaxx returns to the waiting area with a doctor. The ladies and David stand up. "What'd they say?"

Jaxx takes her Mother's hands and holds them tight before she reveals what happened.

"This is doctor Blake Moriel. The paramedics wrote in their report that they reviewed the film from the PAT. They stated that when the PAT arrived to pick up Julz she had a dizzy spell and slipped. When she fell she hit the side of her head on the car. After she didn't respond, PAT called an ambulance. She was barely conscious when the paramedics arrived. When a scan was done of her head the doctor's noticed a slight bleed and a small clot on her brain. I told them to go ahead and drain the clot. They put Julz in a drug induced coma to reduce the swelling."

"*Oh my god!*" Connie exclaims.

Dr. Moriel informs them of other details. "There was some minor swelling, but as far as we can tell there appears to be a tiny bit of manageable brain damage. She was having a hypertensive spike, but we were able to bring down her blood. The blood pressure issue is something we will have to continue to control because apparently she was born with a hole in her heart and the stress from the injury is compromising her cardio health. On top of all of that she has Lupus. We're watching her closely for any changes. As you can imagine things are a pretty tricky treating someone with brain damage, heart damage and Lupus. We will keep her system relaxed to hopefully prevent any systemic flare-ups. She'll be in a drug induced coma for 48 hours. After that we will allow her to wake up on her own. If she doesn't wake up of her own volition, we will take more extensive measures to awaken her."

"Are you saying that she may not wake up?" Jade asks.

"I'm saying that things are tricky with her condition. You may all go in and see her. You can also stay as long as you like." He says.

They all go into the hospital room where they see Julz lying in the bed with medical tubes inserted in her arms and nose. Julz's Mom, Jade, Joe, Daisy and Terra sob softly in the dimly lit room. David stands next to them fighting back tears as he rests his eyes upon the beautiful woman whom he has fallen in love with laying in a hospital bed before him.

Her Mother speaks through tears.

"Julz we love you. You scared us!"

David notices that the monitor registering Julz's heart rate beeps.

"You hear that? You scared me!" Her Mother cries aloud and profusely.

David notices that the monitor beeps again.

This time he notices that the rhythm on the monitor remains steady. He walks over to the side of the bed which is opposite of where her Mother is standing. He gently holds Julz's hand between his hands. Jaxx watches David interact with Julz. She finds it comforting to see the caring affection for her sister in his eyes.

Connie rests her head on the bed next to Julz.

"Mom, I know that you're going to stay here tonight and part of tomorrow. How about you, Joe and Jade take the morning day watch and I'll take the night watch okay?" Jaxx catches David's eyes and gives him a wink and slight nod. He understands that she is communicating that the evening shift will be the best time for his visits so that he can give her distraught mother some room to tend to her sister. Her mother and sisters agree to the arrangement

The next evening Jaxx smooths the way with the shift nurses for David to stay passed visiting hours. He hangs out in the waiting area for Jaxx to finish her visit with Julz. She sends David a text when it's his turn to visit with her sister.

David brings donuts, pizza pastries and signed copies of his books as a thank you gift to the nurses. He also brings a copy of a manuscript of his new horror novel. Watching Julz heart react to the different words that her mother used gave him an idea to use the words from his horror novel to stimulate her heart and mind.

"Julz it's me David. I'm going to stay with you for as long as they will allow me. My brother Ronnie wanted to come and paint your nails, but I wouldn't let him because I have feeling you wouldn't like that. Anyway I brought my new book with me. It's called Prayers of the Wicked. I hope you enjoy it."

David begins to read his novel to Julz. He reads the first two chapters, but monitors barely register a heightened response. He moves on to a more intense part of his book.

"Julz these next parts might get intense so I'm going to hold your hand."

He gently uses his right hand to caress Julz's left hand before he continues reading.

"Del feels the hairs on the back of his neck straighten like little soldiers preparing for battle. He quickly turns to face the menace, but his foe is gone from his sight. Oh, but the Beast is still there quietly watching from a perch in the shadows. Del's heart races inside of his chest because in the reflection of a puddle of ground water, Del is also watching the Beast. And for the first time since Detective Cameron was a rookie, his steely gun hand trembles."

Sure enough the machine monitoring Julz' heartbeat quickens its pace and briefly beeps louder. He continues to read to Julz. Some of the nurses who gathered near the door of Julz's room listen as the award winning writer David Greene reads heart racing parts of his unpublished horror novel to his comatose girlfriend. Jaxx encounters the nurses gathering around her sister's door. She almost shoos them away, but even she gets caught up in the beauty of the spectacle.

The next night David engages in the same routine. He holds Julz's hand as he reads to her. As he moves through the more thrilling parts, not only does Julz respond, but several of the shift nurses gasp aloud when he hits an intense part of the story too.

It's 11pm David kisses Julz on the forehead before finishing his visit with her for the night. He stops in a restroom close very near her room, but he discovers that it's out of order. He wonders through the halls until he finds one a bit of a distance away. As he's walking back from the restroom he over hears two male doctors discussing Julz's care in a partially closed office. He stops to listen.

Physician #1, "Blake said that the Havreaux woman should've come out of the coma by now. He said that he's going to give her a hot shot late tomorrow night to rouse her."

Physician #2, "It's risky with someone who presents with the triple threat of issues that she has; plus, she had a clot. I worry about aggravating her pressure and sparking a brain hemorrhage or heart attack.

Physician #1, "I agree about a vessel bleed, but it's not our call. Blake feels that the risks are minimal.

Physician #2, "*He feels*? That guy acts more like a faith healer than scientist. When is that guy leaving anyway? I heard that his time is up in…"

The doctors stop talking when they think that they hear a noise near the door of the office they are sitting in. David hears the change in the doctor's behavior. He panics and bolts down a nearby stairwell. He runs down to the next level, but the door cannot be opened without a hospital badge. He turns around to return to the floor where Julz is, but it's also locked. He tries every door heading down to the main floor, but finds that they are all locked. Once he gets down to the main floor, a security guard will not allow him to enter the elevators that lead to the floors with the patients on them.

David is scared of what the doctor is planning to do to Julz. He ponders how can't lose another one; someone he cares for, someone he loves. He leaves the hospital in frustration. When he gets home he spends most of the night pacing. He forces himself to get some sleep to try to be fresh for a full day of media events that can't be cancelled. He tries sending Jaxx a message, but he receives no response. Unfortunately, Jaxx keeps left her phone in a hospital scrub room when she was invited to assist with a patient from the emergency room.

The next day David sits for several contracted media engagements. In between interviews he tries to reach Jaxx, but he still can't reach her.

David feels too tired to drive so he arranges for his brother to drive him to the hospital to see Julz.

"Dammit Ronnie that radio interview went too long now it's passed visiting hours. I want to see Julz before they do whatever radical thing the doc is planning to do. I don't know what it is, but I have a strong feeling that I want to see her."

The two brothers sneak into the wing where Julz is sleeping. David sees an unfamiliar nurse heading towards them.

"Excuse me gentleman visiting hours are over. Come back tomorrow between 7am and 7pm." She says.

They keep walking forward anyway. David can see Julz's room.

"Heck her room is right there! It's only six doors away."

"Don't worry bro. I got this. Give me your coat to cover my move. I can probably get you about ten minutes. We'll probably get arrested, so make it count."

"Arrested?"

Ronnie ignores him as he engages the nurse.

"I'm sorry ma'am. I couldn't hear you. Did you say visiting hours are for seven more minutes?" Ronnie says.

"No what I said is that visiting hours are from…"

David quietly slides by her while she is talking to Ronnie.

She notices and yells to David for him to return.

"Sir! Sir!"

But David keeps going. Just as Ronnie tries to ease passed the nurse, she reaches out and grabs his arm. That's when he deploys an underground dance club move called Drop Dead on the Floor.

He screams, "*Ahhhh you tripped me!*" as he quickly falls straight to the floor; landing hard on his back with his left leg and foot bent underneath him.

He lays on the floor uttering soft fakes moans.

"Ohhhh - My back. My leg. Somebody help meh."

The nurse stoops down to his side to examine him.

"*Are you okay sir?*" The nurse asks.

"Ohhhhhh." Ronnie continues his dramatic fake moans.

While his brother distracts the nurse, David makes it to Julz's room. He holds her right hand as he leans in close to speak in her ear.

"Julz I didn't tell you the full story about what happened that day after the helicopter crash. I think that I died that day because I'm missing a piece of time after I was outside of the copter. I remember a voice calling to me to come back and then I remember that my body was shaking violently. You see it wasn't me that was shaking, but it was Youngblood shaking me. He was talking to me and willing me with all of his might to fight; so I did. He said comeback buddy and he shook me. David squeezes Julz's hand tight and then starts to shake her as he speaks in her ear.

"Comeback to me Julz. You're not done yet. You hear me you're not done! Fight baby fight!" He says as he violently shakes her hand.

"Come on and take my hand Julz. I will fight with you! I will fight with you forever! Wakeup Julz and fight! Wake up baby! Hear my voice! Wake up Julz and fight!"

He's now shaking her so hard that her upper body is shuddering too. Suddenly the monitors wildly start to beep. Security guards burst into the room to remove David, but he won't let go of her hand. He won't stop his chant to will Julz back to consciousness; to will her back to life.

Do you hear me Julz? Fight baby! Get up baby! Get up and fight Julz!"

As David is fighting with the guards, something happens. He doesn't see it, but the man sitting in a dark corner of the room partially hidden by a curtain does. It's Uncle Sumner quietly watching over his niece. He abruptly stops cleaning his nails with his large sharp hunting knife. He swiftly leans forward, raises his arm, points his blade at Julz and then shouts –

"Look at the power!"

Everyone snaps their heads towards the voice coming from a dark corner; then quickly traces the hand holding a knife in the direction of Julz. Julz, who is now sitting up in bed with her eyes wide open. She sees men struggling with David. She yells, *"Hey, let David go!"*

She tries to get out of bed to help David, but she is halted by the IV tether in her arm. She looks down at herself in disbelief.

"What the? What's happening? Am I in a hospital?" She shouts.

David yells, "She's back! She's back! Let me go! She's back!"

David jerks his shoulders as he shakes off the guards. He rushes to Julz's side. He gently holds her hand.

"Julz you came back! You scared the crap out of me!"

"Came back from where?" She asks.

"You fell and hit your head."

"I vaguely remember something like that. I was falling and there was a car."

"You've been in a coma for several days ever since you fell and hit your head on the car. I'm so glad you're back."

"A coma huh? It's odd, but I swear that I had a dream where you were calling me; telling me to get up and fight. I remember being pissed and ready to fight; then I woke up in this hospital. Funny huh?"

Yeah, funny." He smiles.

"It seems like you're always there to help me after I fall."

David is about to respond, but he is interrupted when Jaxx and other doctors rush into the room. He is quickly moved to the side as the doctors examine Julz.

"Julz are you okay? How are you feeling? The family is on their way down here."

Julz speaks while yawning. "I feel fine. I just feel really tired. I could use a nap."

Jaxx calls to her sister as she drifts off. "No Julz you need to stay awake. Julz? *Julz?*"

Part Nine

Winter often feels colder than expected in the desert. Some Native people of Arizona believe that as the warmth of all things wane, it is not the time to mourn the loss of the sun. It's a time to embrace beauty wherever they find it. In this they find peace and harmony in what a new season brings.

David can almost hear his own heartbeat.

"Did you get it? It said it's a 9 on the K-Index. He says.

"Yep. The text just came in from the observatory. That's a biggie for sure. I'm grabbing my bag now." She says.

"I'll be there in 15." He says.

"I'll meet you out front." She says

David arrives at the house and Julz jumps in his vehicle.

"Hi babe. Did you pick-up my wet shoes from the new Sporting Goods store?"

"Got em. Oh and the manager said that you won a frozen turkey in a drawing."

"Thanks for getting the shoes. I'll get the turkey later." She says.

"Or I can run it upstairs."

"Oh, you got it. Let's try to hit the road fast so that we can get a good spot. We'll just pack that bird in the snow." She says.

"Roger that!"

Tweedle beep! Tweedle beep!

"Wait. It's Joe going live with an emergency broadcast from the Springs."

"*Juuuuulz!* Are you guys coming? We all dancing nekkid see." Joe slurs into the camera.

Julz and David watch as a blur of faces flash pass the screen.

"We're on our way, but are you guys drunk? You said this is an emergency."

"Woo-hoo! Julz and David are coming. It is an emergent-cee." Joe slurs.

"And no we are not nee-bree-ated." Jade slurs into the camera.

"That's cause we're frickin *drunk! Bwahahahaaha!*" Jaxx slurs into the camera.

"I'm hanging up now." Julz says.

"No wait! I have somethin' to *shell* you." Joe slurs.

Something blocks the image coming in.

"Hey you're breaking up. I can't see you Joe."

"Cause my camera fell on Daisy's nekkid butt. *Bwahahahahaha*! *Happy Holidays!*"

"Good grief!" Julz cuts off the live feed.

"Well I'll never be able to look at Daisy the same way again. Let's roll!" David says.

After driving for only fifteen minutes they can see glimmers of colored lights between the peaks of the mountains. A few more minutes down the road, just passed the higher peaks of the canyon they can finally see one of the most spectacular sight they've ever seen. It's the bright green and red bands of the Aurora Borealis dancing across the southwest sky like giant ribbons in the wind.

They park near the trail leading to one of the dipping areas of the lake sized body of water at Cavern Springs. Luckily the nearby resort installed heated walk paths heading towards the warm water. They stop at the water's edge to admire the magnificence of nature's beauty.

The colorful bands of Aurora Borealis are so bright that they paint the mountains with beautiful waves of light that reveal a frozen water fall with big horned sheep stair stepped along the cliffs in the darkness.

David and Julz are so overcome with joy of being alive to witness so much beauty that they both shed tears.

"Excuse me for drooling." He says as he wipes away a tear.

"Yes we are." Julz says she softly as sobs.

They walk toward the warm water. Julz stumbles, but David catches her before she falls.

"Oops. Sorry about that." She says.

"No need to apologize. In my heart you're perfect. We're perfect."

"You're right David. Hey this is the first time that I've seen your upgraded tatt in person. How do you like it?" She asks.

"I love it. It turned out better than expected." He says.

"Yep and the twelve glow in the dark Air Force Paratroopers fighting glow in the dark zombie bunnies eating bunny brains looks sweet too!" She says.

"What? You guys put glow in the dark Airmen and brain eating zombie bunnies on my back? Ha-ha-ha-ha! That's awesome! I can't wait to see it."

"Yeah I thought the tatt would be a cool reminder of moments we shared during another time before we were perfect."

"Yes, it is." He says.

He sweeps her into his arms. And for the first time their lips meet in a tender kiss. They finally give in to their passion under the dancing colorful lights of the Southern Aurora Borealis. Absolutely perfect!

THE END.

Now que the dancing robot dog. "Hey Abigail!"

Well it's the end of this part of a story, but if you're curious about what kind of dark mystery Del Cameron and Jack Richards have been up to since Wicked Prayers; catch up with them on the next page in a short story called Black Widow.

Black Widow

It's a cool winter morning in Flagstaff, Arizona. Detectives Del Camron and Jack Richards drive from the airport to a crime scene in the city. Del is in the driver's seat.

"Hey Jack how are things going during week-three of babysitting your sister's kid? Is he giving you and Soummer any ideas to have one of your own?" Del asks.

"Um no. That five-year old has more energy than a jack rabbit."

"You should give him one of those Adventures of PJ and Split Pea activity books. It'll keep him busy for hours."

"Okay, I'll check that out. Hey look we're here." Jack says.

Buzz-Buzz-Buzz! Buzz-Buzz-Buzz! Del's phone alerts him to new text messages, but he ignores them.

"I don't know why T.U.R.F. sent us on this case. Agent Sherman said it may be related to a deceased truck driver that was found on the edge of town, but that seems like average crime stuff." Del says

"I thought that victim had a wound consistent with an ice pick attack. That should be a local precinct matter; not something in our other worldly lane." Jack says.

"Oh I pray that this *is* in our lane." Del says.

"Man you have some wicked prayers Del."

"Nah – I'm just tired of sitting around for several weeks between cases."

Buzz-Buzz-Buzz!   Buzz-Buzz-Buzz! Del's receives more text message alerts.

"Man your phone is really blowing up." Jack says.

"It's my Uncle Shelby's nurse. Just before we boarded the plane she sent me a message about an agreement during a state of emergency. I sent her a text that I'd get to it once I returned to Autumntown, but she has been texting me like a crazy person ever since.

"Hahaha! Shelby getting punished for sneaking into the pantry after hours again?" Jack asks.

"The way she's been blowing up my phone, I think this is a whole lot worse than pudding theft." Del says.

The detectives pull up in front of the Western Pines Motel. Two local police cars and a coroner's wagon are on the scene. A police officer waves them over. Del reads the guy's name tag.

"Hello Officer Adams. I'm Detective Camron and this Detective Richards." He and Jack show the officer their badges and IDs.

The officer nods for them to follow him to a motel room.

"You guys got here quick. We were told not to move the officer's body until you arrived."

"We didn't know the victim is a cop." Jack says.

The detectives enter the motel room.

"Yeah he transferred from Washington a few months ago." Adams says.

"What's his name Officer?" Jack asks

Del stares at the softly wrinkled face of the naked man lying in the bed before responding. "It's Ed Gallagher!"

"Holy crap it is him! He even has a tatt that says, Autumntown Stronger!" Jack says.

"I take it that you were friends with the officer?" Adams asks.

"He risked his life to help my family. The poor bastard. I deeply owed the guy for what he did for me. Where is the ice pic wound?" Del asks.

"Ice pick? The Coroner did a quick exam and it turns out he died of a spider venom induced heart attack."

"Spider venom? Clearly our folks got their wires crossed." Del says.

"See the raised bluish veiny area spreading from the right side of his groin, thigh and stomach area?"

"Yeah."

"He's the third victim that we've found that looked like this. All three men had the same poison patch on them, but this is the first person doing the decaying thing."

"Yeah, I thought it was odd that he looks much older than he should. You guys identify what kind of spider venom this is?" Del asks.

"Black Widow."

"Black Widow?" Del responds.

"Yeah, she mates and she…" Adams begins.

"I got that. It's just that most adults don't die from Widow bites; especially not like this." Del says.

"Nope." Adams says.

"Did all three guys die at this motel?" Jack asks.

"Two guys died in their homes. One on the west side of town and the other on the south side. We are on the north side.

And before you ask, we didn't find any drugs or foreign DNA on the other two vics. We haven't checked Officer Gallagher yet." Adams says.

"Any evidence of condom usage?" Del asks.

"None." Adams replies.

"What about his patrol partner? There must've been something shared about who the decedent was seeing or his favorite hook up fishing spots." Del says.

"We spoke with Officer Obu, but he wasn't aware of his partner seeing anyone. He didn't know of any places that the vic may have frequented on a regular basis. Our suspicion is that this was from a random hook up." Adams says.

"What about surveillance? This place have any cameras?" Jack asks.

"Um, it has a reputation of being one of those no-tell motels. If you know what I mean? One person picks up the key at the desk and then sneaks their honey dip into the room. It's the kind of place where no one wants any witnesses of their dirty deeds." Adams says.

"It's sounds like a criminal's dream lodge; but it gives us a clue that whomever the officer saw, he preferred to keep it on the low and rent a room in this joint than to take the person back to his home." Jack says.

"That's a good point Jack. It could've been a fetish or infidelity thing, but it still doesn't shed light on the insect mystery. Either only Black Widow spiders in Flagstaff evolved into right sided groin biters of men or this is something else. Do you have a picture of the bite on you? I want to get a closer look at the wound." Del says.

"You can just lift up his..." Adams says.

Del interrupts him. "Hey I'm usually not squeamish, but I prefer not to handle my buddy's little buddy period."

"Ditto." Jack says.

Officer Adams rolls his eyes.

"Oh for the love of - thank goodness I'm wearing gloves." Adams says before lifting the deceased officer's little buddy.

"That's a very large wound that looks like it goes beneath the surface skin and into the groin." Del says.

"The other vics had wounds about a half inch deep too."

"Ouch! The wound is almost shaped like a curved triangle. If it were a spider bite, wouldn't there be two or more wounds?" Del asks.

"Yep." Adams says.

"It's the size of the injury that's throwing me off. No spider could've done that. I was thinking that someone likely used a needle, but I've never seen one shaped like that." Jack says.

"There lies the Black Widow mystery gentleman. I heard this is right in your lane." Adams says.

"It's starting to look like it is." Del says.

Del and Jack leave the motel. They drive over to local Bistro for a bite to eat. The hostess leads the detectives to a booth and gives them menus.

Jack notices a faraway look in Del's eyes. He's knows it well. It's the look of thinking too hard about hard stuff.

"It's a shame about Gallagher. That death cloud from Autumntown spreads like root-rot in a dark forest. This whole thing is making me feel kind of twitchy; like I need to hit the shooting range pronto! Screw it! How about them Eagles?"

In his uncomfortable state between rage and sadness, Del uses their code for let's change the subject and Jack understands.

"It's pretty nice having this mega money T.U.R.F. dining card huh? It sure beats eating that cheap grub we get in Autumntown." Jack says.

"I love that cheap grub. I really miss the smells of hot grease, coffee and donuts swirling through the air of Dave's Greasy Spoon. Man that aroma reminds me of simpler ti…"

Del stops abruptly. He has that certain glint in his eyes that he gets when his idea of a breath takingly beautiful woman catches his attention. Jack is familiar the look on his Del's face, but he can't see the woman coming up the aisle from his rear. He casually watches Del watch her as she approaches him. Now he catches the aroma of her intoxicating perfume. In another step Jack sees her side profile and rear end as the sexy woman wearing all black slowly passes by their table. She drops a black silk scarf with the pattern of a red hour glasses on it. Del begins to bend down to pick it up, but a guy at the table next to theirs snatches it up and hands it to the black haired woman. He starts to chat her up.

"Too slow Del. You're starting to lose your step man."

"Be still my heart! That dark hair, those ruby red lips; plus, she is wearing that dress like a glove. Oh well. I guess it wasn't meant to be." Del says.

"Frankly I wouldn't be too quick to hook up in this town. At least not until we figure out what's going on."

"Well what's *not* going on is anything to do with an ice pick." Del says.

"I've been thinking about that ever since we left the motel. Something tells me that the truck driver they found on the edge of Autumntown with a hole in his heart doesn't have anything to do with an ice pick either." Jack says.

"I'm right there with you man. It bugged me from the beginning that the trucker's crime scene was too clean. Where was the spilled blood from that truck driver's pumping heart? Anyway Jack, what do you think could've made a wound like that on Gallagher?"

"I don't know. Maybe a huge, one fanged Black Widow spider with a jones for the right side of man beef."

"Ugh! Why'd you have to throw beef out there like that when I'm about to eat?"

"Hey, you can always order their special."

"What's that?"

"Andouille sausage and two eggs."

"Stop it." Del tries not to laugh. He cracks a muted smile.

"Make sure that you get the shrimp and grits, but you have to watch out for the shrimp though."

"Why?" Del asks.

"You gotta make sure they've been dee-veined."

"See Jack, you play too much.

Now que the dancing robot dog."

Afterword from the Author

I hope that you enjoyed Before We Were Perfect. Although this is a fictional story, I had David Green share the story about an Air Force aviation accident actually happened in 1998 at Nellis AFB, Nevada. Here's why I was inspired to write about it.

In 1986 I joined the Air Force initially as Club and Recreation Manager. However, about a year into my career I received training in a secondary duty to recover human remains from major accidents. I eventually was trained in mortuary affairs to learn how to care for personal effects, finger print and foot print the deceased as well as where to store remains.

In 1997, while I was stationed at Nellis Air Force Base my boss gave a Thanksgiving dinner at her house. She invited members from our office and her friends Captain Karl Youngblood and his wife. This was my boss' first attempt at cooking a turkey and it was an epic fail. I'm talking browned bird on the outside with a forgotten frozen giblet bag melting on the inside. I stepped in to help fix the culinary mess, but it was so hot in the house I had to step outside to cool off. Captain Youngblood happened to be standing outside too. We ran through the whole series of where you from and what do you do questions. He said, "I'm from Michigan." I said, me too. He said, "I went to college in West Virginia." I said, that's where one of my parents is from. He said, one of his parents is from West Virginia too. I was like, man that's freaky. Next you'll tell me that you're an Aries. He said, "I am. My birthday is at the end of March." I said shut up! I'm a March Aries too. He said, "Okay that really is freaky."

After the holidays we'd run into each other several times a week. We'd crack jokes or generally shoot the crap and then go our separate ways. He or his wife would stop by our section regularly to say hi or do some business. Sometimes he'd quickly poke his head in my office, make a funny face and wave hello before darting off. On Sep 2nd 1998, I spoke with Captain Youngblood while we stood outside of the Customer Support building. We were joking around about the upcoming Thanksgiving. He said, "It's almost that time of year again." I said yes I know, but I know where I'm not having dinner. He said, "I'm with you on that one. You guys (people from my office) can always have dinner at my commander's house. You can make the pie. I loved your sweet potato pie." I said, thanks, but maybe we can all get together in town. He said, "That'll be good. I'm going on a deployment. We have plenty of time to figure it out, but whatever we do, we can't let your boss do any of the cooking." We laughed and then went our separate ways.

On Sep 3rd, around 4:00 am I received a phone call from my office that I had to come into work on a "real world recall." That meant something bad happened. I arrived at work before sunrise. I was informed that there was an aviation accident near Nellis AFB. For the first time in my career I was called to go out to a site and recover the remains of the fallen. I prepared myself to go and see the unthinkable. I asked what squadron was impacted. That's when I was informed that twelve guys from the 66th Rescue Squadron were killed and that my bud Captain Karl Youngblood was among the deceased. I was overcome with grief for the loss of so many brothers in arms and for the loss of my buddy who I joked around with several hours before he died. Sadly, due to health reasons related post Iraq brain damage I was told to stand down during the initial part of the recovery. I have been filled with deep regret about that day ever since. In the moment when I was finally called on to perform the most sacred part of my duties I was unable to serve my friend. I wish that I could've helped them all.

I created what must've been a horrific experience during the final moments of the accident. However, all of the specifics about what the crew went through during those last moments are not fully known. Although I created two survivors from the chopper accident in Before We Were Perfect, in reality all twelve souls perished that day. I wrote the accident into the story because this tragedy should not be forgotten. I also did it as a dedication to my buddy Captain Karl P. Youngblood: Pilot, warrior, newlywed, homeboy and a really cool dude.

I also shared some of the real life mishaps that I experienced while living with a combination of brain damage, a hole in my heart and Lupus. What is Lupus? Lupus is an autoimmune disease that is NOT contagious. It super boosts the immune system to overreact and attack heathy areas of the body even though nothing is wrong. At times it can be life threatening. However, I decided long ago to face my basket full of challenges by continuing to fight on with a little humor in my heart.

Here are few more facts:

- **Bunny face down in the snow:** Yes, I had a spell and fell down outside in the snow. I shooed away the person who tried to help me up because I was still having the spell. When I looked around me there was a bunny staring at me in the snow.

- **Numb butt:** Yes, I have had and still do experience intermittent numbness in my butt and limbs.

- **Why aren't there pics of the helicopter sequence?** If this were a movie I would've directed it differently. However, in print, I wanted readers to imagine what David is saying just like Julz would have to imagine it. I felt that printed pictures would weaken the impact of the scene.

- **Being shaken in a hospital bed while unconscious during an emergency:** I experienced a similar scene of someone shaking and willing me back to consciousness while I was in a hospital bed. Oh Lord he was shaking me. The person who did it was a military doctor, but I don't know his name. For years I've tried to find out who he is so that I can thank him for his compassionate care, but to this day I still don't know his name. It's on my bucket list to find him.

- **Trapped in a prepper's house:** Yes, in the 80s I was trapped in a paranoid guy's overly fortified house after he passed out. That's why Joe is wearing an 80s Halloween costume.

- **Why is the title of the story David Green read to Julz called Night of the Leapers?** It is what I was originally going name my international award winning novel Wicked Prayers.

- **Why a tattoo shop?** I decided to go with a tattoo shop because 1) I wanted my characters to be artistic and 2) a few of my family members who received large tattoos were told to see their doctor if there were any problems. I thought to myself that it would be cool if all tattoo artists were medically certified and they had an urgent care and in-patient recovery section at their tattoo shop.

- **Why Cajun?** My son-in-law is a very vocally proud man from the Bayou. His love for Cajun country inspired me.

- **Uncle Sumner:** He is a character based on a deceased relative.

- **Why Flagstaff?** I've driven through Flagstaff a few times. I love the majestic beauty of the mountains surrounding the city. I was always surprised by how cold it gets there.

- **Why the Aurora Borealis in Arizona?** I've experienced the magical beauty of the Northern Lights many times while living in Alaska, but one time I caught the Southern Lights while driving through Arizona so I thought that it would be cool to write about it

- **Why "J" names?** My father used to call an aunt who used to baby sit me Jaxx. I thought that it would be cute to give all of the siblings "J" names.

- **Why sisters?** As a formerly doting oldest sister, I'm familiar with the dynamics between sisters.

Resources

Below are some resources for people managing Lupus, wounded warriors; plus, something for Aurora Borealis enthusiasts in Arizona.

Wounded Warriors
Veterans Crisis Line: 1-800-273-8255
https://www.va.gov/vso/VSO-Directory.pdf

Lupus
https://medlineplus.gov/MS.html

City of Flagstaff, Arizona
http://flagstaff.az.gov/

National Oceanic Atmospheric Administration's K-Index
http://www.swpc.noaa.gov/products/planetary-k-index

Bonus Picks

Before We Were Perfect

A

Dramedy

By Award Winning Author
S.D. Moore
Illustrated by Kostovski Nikola